Blessing Road

By

Adventor Trye

PublishAmerica
Baltimore

First printing

Softcover 978-1-4489-2497-4
PUBLISHED BY PUBLISHAMERICA, LLLP
www.publishamerica.com
Baltimore

Printed in the United States of America

Dedicated to our mothers:

Yamah KwetaYardoe and Kiapeh Tokpa,

No child can forget your unconditional maternal love

A divine orator once reminded his hearers,
"…Inasmuch as you did not do it to one of the least,
you did not do it to me. Behold, I come quickly;
and my reward is with me, to give every man
according to his works."
Matt 25: 45, Rev 22:12

Chapter 1

Suah was worried. Nearly ten years had passed since she had given birth to a child. Her name had become the latest gossips in the ten-hut village of Payeta. The rebuttals to their mockery remained in her mind unspoken. She continued to gratify the Lord and her ancestors in her dilemma as she held on to her stunned marriage with Yallon.

Coming from a small size family and as a man from Leewah Country who believed in their tradition, Yallon wanted more children. From birth, he had been taught that having more children was a special blessing from the Lord, because none of the villagers knew which child could survive from the various tropical and childhood diseases to become their breadwinner. He had seen most of his age-mates, including Mualon and Waluma, already had the number of children they needed by their many wives and concubines.

Even though having more children was their ethical belief, Yallon had vowed to remain committed to his one wife and to have the number of children the Supreme Power could give him.

The fetish priests, in fact, had assured Yallon of having at least another child if his wife would submit to him, to stop eating animals offered to idols, and to stop bathing alone outside during the silent night.

Suah did not want to inflame the shaky condition of her marriage. Neither did she want a curse from the supreme leader nor the genie that passed through the village during the quiet hours of the night. She immediately began to eat the right kind of meats and to bath early indoors. Her romantic life flourished with her husband and brought them closer than ever before.

Suah appeared strong and healthy. She still maintained her beauty in her middle age. Her husband loved her, especially when she braided her hair with two-plaits and wore the bunch of colorful beads around her neck, while the inscribed alligator tattoo glittered on her skin.

Now, in addition to her delay in bringing forth a child, several months had passed since Suah lastly received her monthly assignment. Her mind was not free about contracting a disease. She was curious of knowing what had actually gone wrong with her system. As she frequently consulted her few female friends and the herbalists, they always told her that perhaps that was an early sign of her menopause. She appeared extremely bothered; but, she continued to live by her faith and prayer.

Finally, in the process of time, one night came as a busy night. The women had been running in and out of the little bush, which surrounded the big cotton tree behind the hut of Mama Yatta, the youngest widow of Chief Bada Paye, the founder of the village situated by the bank of Wuo Creek. The children and the young women remained indoors. The men were kept on the alert for any eventuality, and for any assistance that would be needed from them.

By the late noon of October 12, 1977, Neh Korto, the head midwife, came out, informing Yallon and the other men that Suah had given birth to a child, a beautiful girl.

Yallon was bulged with the greatest satisfaction in his life. He brought out several bottle gourds of fresh palm wine, the locally produced beverage, for the people who were present to celebrate the good news. He was happy that he had gotten four children, the minimum number of children he had ever wished for.

Even his frends, Mualon and Waluma as well as Qualilon and Dedalah, led the jubilant crowd, running around the village, pouring some of the palm wine everywhere, chanting in the Kpelle vernacular with his name.

Yallon is now the real man!
Yallon has become as one of us;
The Lord has blessed Yallon with children.
Four is the number Yallon always wanted;
Four is the perfect number for men.
Four is the blessed number for children;
Children are our greatest legacy.
Yallon is now the real man!

Before the day could end, most of the people were exhaustedly drunk as the men continued to bring liquors of all kinds to celebrate the day.

On the eighth day, the people of Payeta again joined the couple to dedicate the child to the Lord and their ancestors. Neh Korto, who was also the mother of Suah, stretched the baby upward and chanted, "Nah Allah, here is your child. Please bestow your blessings upon her."

Three times she lifted the child up to the sky. Then, she blew her breath on the baby and informed the people who were present, "The Lord has already blessed her."

She named the child "Latto," meaning, "Make the name known." Taking the child to be a special person, Neh Korto perceived that one day Latto would grow up and become powerful among men and women, traveling to many places, learning the lifestyles of others, and making the name of Payeta known to the outside world.

But, Suah preferred calling her child "Marlah," meaning, "Just for the name's sake." She was referring to the attitude of her husband who always wanted more children, but he could not support the ones he already had. She complained that her husband's attitude always changed after the birth of each child. This time again, Yallon had refused to stop his irresponsible behavior as he promised.

Just a few days after her recent delivery, she saw Yallon, spending much time with friends, smoking tobacco, drinking palm wine and cane juice, instead of looking for a job at the nearby rubber plantations or producing some palm oil to support his family. Suah was not only bothered by the troubling behavior of her husband, but the mockery that came from people who did not like people who lived sluggishly in the village.

However, a few years later, Suah was proud to see Latto, growing up according to the tradition of their ancestors. Besides fixing fishing nets and baskets, Latto had learned how to farm, fish, cook, and clean around the hut. She had learned all the etiquettes and norms as well as the trainings prescribed for women of Leewah.

Since Suah could occasionally become the main source of incomes for the home, each day, she persuaded Latto to join her cut down trees and burn them for charcoal. From the sale of the charcoal, they supported themselves like other women, who had no other means of support, were doing.

On that morning of 1988, Latto had accompanied Suah to sell their charcoal along the main motor-road that connected all regions of Leewah. She had on no footwear and the brown dust from the unpaved motor-road had taken up places amongst her toes. She had a little piece of red and black cloth wrapped around her waist, and another placed around her chest. A white cosmetic chalk had been rubbed across her forehead, around her jaws and under her chin as was tradition.

Latto was at least a yard behind her mother when they began to hear the whirling beats of the teaching hospital's generator. Feeling plagued by fatigues, she could no longer maintain her strength. The twenty-five pound bag of charcoal had buried her head in her shoulders, while the heat from the morning sun drained her body of moisture.

Still, Latto pretended to behave strong, and she did not want Suah to detect what was happening to her. She called to her mother and promised to follow her in order for them to sell their goods before the sunset.

"I'm glad you know that," her mother said. "You know charcoal is the only lucrative business for us (women) in this place. Since we have no other income, we will continue to make more charcoal for those who are unable to fix it."

The sun was overhead, and the Muslim mid-day prayer call had already been made. Suah seemed to be somehow discouraged, because no one had bought any of their goods since morning.

She said, "It seems like our Lord is sleeping over our business today."

Latto quickly interrupted her, "How can you say that, Mommy?"

Her mother rebuked her, "I don't have to tell you what you want to hear. Not every day you expect good luck to come to you. We have passed many villages; no one has bought any of our goods. I'm sure the people around here have bought all their supplies from the sellers who came before us."

With a groaning voice, Latto answered her mother again, "Maybe this is not as bad a day as you think. If we even cut all the trees from the entire nation, the people around here have to kindle their fire, press their clothes, heat themselves, and cook their food, they will always look for more charcoal to buy."

As Latto was becoming inaudible by the weight of the load, Suah discovered that it wasn't the normal voice of her daughter. When she looked back, she saw her standing, sweating and in tears.

"No! Latto," she said. "You need to rest. This load is weighing you down. Let's relax under this palm tree so that you can regain your strength.

"I'm sorry, my child. I know you might also be hungry. We didn't eat any food this morning before coming on this trip.

"Anyway, don't worry, when we go home, we will have a nice meal, honey." Suah tried to engage her daughter into a friendly conversation after placing their loads on a little heap by the roadside.

This time, Suah directed her daughter to see the nightingale, the dodo, and the pigeon birds, chirping in the sky, while the squirrels and the lizards were running around the palm tree above them. She marveled that the Lord had made the animals special to fetch for their livelihood first before going on to play during their spare hours. "Learning from the animals is a valuable lesson for us, human beings," she said. "We must always strive for what we need before doing anything else. Quitting is always a defeat for the quitter. Those who give up or give in have a limited opportunity to maintain their personal well-beings or to contribute to the development of their society. There are billions of chances always available for the resilient people and those who seek them."

Suah continued, "Latto, whatever you put your mind to in this world, is what you get at the end. There is no magic about any man's success, once you do correctly and on time what your mind tells you to do or your official duty as a human being, the Lord will surely bless it. As my mother always tells me, 'Self-defeat is the weapon that kills the coward many times before his day of confrontation. Even, procrastination makes the sluggard to sleep with an empty stomach in an untidy bed.' Before a man succeeds in this world, he must have many teardrops."

After laying herself flat on the ground to straighten her sore neck, Latto, said to her mother, "I hear all of that. But, did you know that my birthday was Wednesday a few days ago?"

"Yeah, I know!" Suah jokingly said as she rolled up her eyebrows at her daughter and smiled. "That means you are running towards being a woman, and you will soon have children who will be bothering me for their care and support, again."

Latto behaved like an angry tropical baboon. "I'm not thinking about children, Mommy! I'm talking about my education. I'm now eleven years old, and we have entered another new year. Yet, I haven't been to school." Latto wept as she pursued an ant with her index finger on the log that she sat on. She looked up into her mother's face with a childlike gaze and said, "Please promise me that I will go to school this year. Please, Mama."

Latto's mother became very agitated about the demand and vented her anger at her. "My dear, how can I promise you that? Where will the money come from if I promise you this? In fact, there's no school in this place. How will you go to school? "You must tell me! Do you see your brother, Jucuma? He hasn't been to school for the same reason. As for you and your sisters, I'm not worried about you, because it doesn't matter if our women do not attend the white man's school. Completing our traditional training is the greatest task for all women, I am happy that you have already done yours."

She continued, "The white man's education belongs to them or men from the privileged class; not for the struggling men. It is the responsibility of the privileged men as well as the poverty stricken men to bear burdens of their wives and other female relatives. Any assistance from women in general, as I'm doing for you along with your siblings, is an added blessing, not a right for men, including your father."

Lotta retorted, "That isn't the case in this world nowadays, Mommy. The world is teaching all women to be well-educated and independent. The world cannot succeed without the inputs of women. Parents are obligated to educate all their children both girls and boys.

"Several nearby villagers are sending their girls and boys to school. Very soon their villages will be developed, while ours remains underdeveloped. Seeing white women as doctors, teachers or missionaries should teach you a valuable lesson. I don't think the Lord told the white men to educate all their children, while he told the black men to educate boys or none, making them to appear in society as troublemakers, baggers, immoral or non-compliant people."

Suah yelled, "Well, I'm not going to continue arguing with you today. You must tell your liquor sucking father to send you to the world-class school you want." Suah excuse herself. She did not want to give the young lass any false hope when she didn't have the means to underwrite the cost.

"You know that I'm not used to Daddy. In fact, who wants to smell his oozy liquor odor, or to hear the sound of the cussing bomb that comes out of his uncontrolled mouth?" Latto joined her mother to condemn her father as a way of convincing her.

Suah giggled at her and said, "Well, that's you and your father's business. All I want you to know is that your age cannot allow you to stay away from me or to walk forty-five miles every day to school in Jamesburg or Lewisville."

Latto still pressed on with her demand. "But you can find someone nice around there to help me with lodging. Many good people know that there is nothing better than doing good things for others who are struggling for means to survive."

"That is not true," her mother disputed. "Let me tell you something, little girl! Nobody can do better things for you more than your own parents. Human beings are the most selfish animals on this earth. They always protect and provide for their own and use others as their preys."

"You can't make that kind of blunt statement about others. At least, there are some people who sacrifice their lives for others. And why must you overlook the fact that you don't want to find reasons to allow me to be the person I want to be?"

"Don't you think I know what I'm talking about?" Suah asked.

"Well, you don't have to be angry with me. I may not know what you know. But I just want you to understand that they don't have to be nice like you. The little assistance I would get from them would help me, but especially you and our village in the future. I'm not going to remain under your care forever. And I don't want you to continue suffering in your old age. That is why God blessed you to have so many children. You don't know which of us will become the head rooster to protect and provide for us or to fight against any invading rooster. You know that the condition of the world is changing everyday. No one wants to remain as the loser or as the habitual servant to the strong. Grandma always says that God has given all of us an equal opportunity, but striving harder to achieve your aspiration makes you more successful several steps ahead of others." Latto's eyes watered as she talked with her mother.

"Look, Latto! The raccoon knows its throat before making the attempt to swallow palm nuts. You know what you are talking about. What I am thinking about right now is for us to reach to the hospital compound. Perhaps, we will be lucky to find someone there to buy our goods. I'm worrying about the two days that are left. You know that on next Monday, the scheduled thirty-woman working group will work on our rice farm."

As a leader, the workers expected Suah to feed them with enough food and liquor. Some even planned to go earlier along with the salsa and drum players on the eve-night of the workday to her house to start their enjoyment. She had one living goat and a few pieces of red deer meat now on hand for the workers.

Latto still paid less attention to her mother's utterances. She said, "I'm always worried about the future." She sighed as if this was the greatest disappointment in her life and said, "Who else could I turn to if my mother of all women has failed me?"

Her mother glared at her. "What do you know about the future? You talk as if to say you know it all. You don't have to feel that way; it is only that you don't know the work of the Lord. Your opportunity will come when the time has come for you one day."

Latto asked her mother, "When is it ever going to be some day? When is it ever going to be my opportunity when I'm getting older everyday?

"Can't you understand that since the pioneers brought western education, there has been no female in our family who has learned how to read and write? When will we have one? Look around and see others, educating their children every year. This should be a big disgrace for our family. Are you worried about that?"

Suah roared again, "Calm down, young lady! I'm not going to allow you to go on with all your silly talk! I'm doing my best for you everyday. Do you want to pay me with ungratefulness? Do you want to be unkind like your father? Let's close the chapter on such talk right now, I mean now!"

"I am sorry about that!" She quickly apologized to find a common ground with her mother.

Looking at Latto regretfully, Suah then left the log she sat on and came up with an apologetic approach to the dispute. "Well, we can't spend the whole day arguing when we are supposed to be relaxing. Stand up and let me lay the bag on your head. We do not have a time to relent until we find someone to buy our goods today."

"Which bag are you talking about? Do you think I am able to move my legs again? My neck is still sore, Mommy."

"Yes, you are! What do you mean by you are unable to move your legs? You don't want to say that. You must make haste and follow me, now, right now. I say!"

"Eh huh, how long do we still have to go?"

"From here to Jamesburg, to Lewisville, anywhere our legs lead us today."

Overlooking the reality that Latto was in a terrible pain, Suah said, "That was one of the reasons I didn't want you to follow me this morning. I knew you could be my problem today."

"Why did you want to walk alone?" Latto asked. "Have you not heard that there are bunch of heart-men along almost every bush-road in this land? Many people, including Giddings, have disappeared and no one actually knows their whereabouts. I can't afford to miss you like that, Mama."

"God forbids it," her mother replied.

As young as she was, Latto told her mother that whenever it was the time for general elections in Leewah, many devious politicians always carried on some sort of ritualistic killing of innocent people to make juju with their body-parts in order for them to win their contested positions.

Then Suah replied to Latto, "So, can you free me from the hands of your killers?"

"Not exactly as you said!" Latto replied. "But when a person like me is around you, talking with you, the assailants would be frightened, assuming that there are many people traveling with you."

"Well then, Miss Guarding Angel! Since you came along to guard me from the hands of your presumed murderers, then wake up. Let's go. You can continue to guard me like you were guarding Chief Dokpa Jao in Payeta."

Later, Suah realized that she was somehow dealing harshly with her daughter. She changed her mannerism. She discovered that they had tramped quicker than they had ever thought of. Besides, she also realized that Latto had not gotten over the gruesome pain from the thorn that pierced her left foot on the day before.

Suah came up with an accommodating opinion and said, "I know, Latto. I know. You have the mind. You are right that you want to be somebody. You too must be educated according to the white man's way.

"Thanks, Mon!" Latto quickly interrupted and hugged her mother.

Then, Suah continued, "Anyway, don't worry. We will discuss your concern some day. If there is a God for us, He will surely provide the means for your education like He did for Kiamu Kelikow, my kidnapped brother, Jimmy's son, who is somewhere in the white man's world."

Again, Latto burst up with a smile, appreciating her mother's decision. And her mother joined her to celebrate the compromise.

Chapter 2

From the balcony of the colonial-style building surrounded by mango and almond fruit trees, stood Manu still dressed in her school uniform. Manu was the daughter of Dr. Frula Kiamu, an administrator and Mrs. Leemu Kiamu, a nurse of the Christian Hospital and School of Nursing situated between Jamesburg and Lewisville in the Central Province of Leewah.

Manu was surprised to see a little girl, struggling under a certain load, following a lady who seemed to be her mother. Manu came down the staircase to get a better glimpse of her.

While looking on, Manu wondered why the lady must allow the little girl to carry that kind of heavy load. She thought her mother was also watching what was happening on the road.

As Manu's heart pounded with compassion, she said again, "I'm sure my mother can do something about this. I can persuade her to buy those items just for the sake of that little girl. Even though we don't know them, we must help them somehow for God's sake."

Manu turned around to locate her mother, who was busy, preparing the family lunch on the porch, overlooking the catfish pond valley. Leemu, too, couldn't figure out why her daughter continued to look at the approaching lady and her daughter. She somehow concluded that Manu was interested in the people's business as a way of avoiding helping her with the cooking.

Leemu called Manu's attention, "You, young lady, go in and take off that uniform. Your school is closed. You don't have to keep it on the whole day. And, you must hurry up and come help me. Maybe you are not hungry, but Numeh and I are hungry."

As Manu and her mother were talking, they saw the approaching little girl bump her wounded foot against the dried earth. She screamed. "I'm dying, Mommy!" She staggered under the load and it fell from her head.

The suffering girl was Latto with her mother, Suah.

Suah quickly rushed to Latto and placed the load back on her head without checking or asking what was going wrong with her. Latto, too, did not tell her Mom about her problem, but she continued to grunt sadly, considering her action to be merciless.

Her mother began to calm her, "You will be fine. Let's go. Don't be lazy, my young woman. You will have much more difficult things to experience than this."

As Latto hopped under the load, the scene once again caught the attention of Manu and she screamed, "Oh! Mommy, see what is happening across the road."

"Like what?" her mother asked.

"Across the street is a little girl, suffering under a heavy load. She can't take a step. I'm so worried about her.

"Please, Mommy. Can you buy the goods they are selling for the sake of that little girl?"

"I don't think I stayed home today to be bothered by your many unnecessary requests," Leemu said.

"Please Mommy, do it just for my sake. You know Mommy, if I were the one under that load; you would expect someone to assist me. Right?"

"Do you know those people?" Leemu asked.

"No! I don't have to. You shouldn't, either."

"In every case you want me to be a Samaritan. You can care for people, but not to take on their problems," said Leemu, lowering the pitch of her voice as she went closer to her daughter. She didn't want any repeat of such a talk.

Manu said, "People know you and what you can do. I don't think you can easily hide yourself from the truth. You don't have to know them. In this case, you can be their Samaritan today. I am sure you can do it as you usually do, Mommy."

Leemu reluctantly looked at her daughter and said, "Then, do what you think is right. I am not here for that." She continued to prepare her food.

As Manu began to shout, Latto and Suah heard her. They looked across the road and saw a little girl, standing by the banister waving and calling them to come with the loads.

Suah smiled with hope and enthusiasm.

"Who says our God will continue to sleep? If he was sleeping, now, he has wakened up to bless us," she said. "It is not every drop of bathing water that gets on the skin. If these people are our potential buyers, we will give them the little bag as a way of persuading them to buy the big one. Doing that is better than to carry the whole charcoal back to the village without getting a thing for my scheduled working group," she stated.

Suah and Latto allowed the van to pass with the nursing students who were going to the dining hall for lunch after giving vaccinations against childhood diseases in Belema. They looked again down the road to give ways to the other approaching motors. When they saw that the place was cleared, they quickly crossed the road and reached the place where the voice had come from.

When they reached at the basement of the building, they saw a big German shepherd on a chain at the entrance. They hesitated to take any step further.

"I can't move from this place," Latto said as she dropped her load and maintained an ample space away from the barking dog. (She hadn't forgotten the death of Mentar from the bite of a dog that was infested with the rabies virus in Payeta a few years ago).

Also feeling frightened by the gaze of the dog, Suah directed her daughter, "Please pass against the wall where the chain on the dog will not reach and come to me."

As Leemu stood on the porch along with her eleven-year-old daughter, Manu, carefully watching them, she encouraged, "Don't be afraid, Shepherd doesn't bother people. Please climb the stairs this way on to the porch."

But they were still frightened to take their steps.

Then, Leemu quickly reached down to them and took the bag the little girl had dropped and led them upstairs.

As she squatted to open one of the bags, Leemu asked, "I hope the charcoal is good. Some of the charcoal some people produce can't make a fire blaze very well."

"I know it is not easy to work for money. I always make sure to produce a good quality of charcoal for sale. A wise person doesn't allow any mischief in a business, which always brings abundant curses," said Suah with a gutted mind.

"I was just kidding," Leemu said as she quickly noticed Suah's changed mood. "I know most of our older people always do good business unlike most of our younger ones who always want quick money from bad business deeds."

She asked again, "How much do you sell them?"

"Ten dollars! But you can give me eight dollars for all. The little bag is your bonus."

"Oh no! Why can't I buy them with the full price?"

"I just want to build a line of friendship with you, Ma'am."

Suah feared losing her first customer for the day. She knew that if the goods weren't bought, they could carry everything back to the village, and that could be a big setback for her rice farming.

"Building a friendship doesn't mean that you should cheat yourself. I know you have come to sell your goods for money to keep your farming on time."

"Yes, Ma'am," Suah replied. "In fact, we are already late for farming this year."

"So, should you encourage me to exploit you just for the sake of friendship?"

"No, Ma'am. That's our way of encouraging our customers for tomorrow. Through this, our customers would want to continue business with us."

"That's a wrong business tactic. I see why our standard of living in this region has always made us to appear poor. We are so kind until we lose all our resources; sometimes our credibility is abused by people who like free things. They usually take us to be their gold creek, where they usually come to dig theirs. Anyway, I purposely called you for this small bag of charcoal. My daughter was crying for it when she saw your little girl, dragging behind you. We have enough charcoal. My husband bought charcoal this morning from some women."

"I'm sure they might have been my sisters-in-law. Nowah and Yamah. They told me last night that they were coming to Jamesburg to sell their charcoal. Well, I'm thankful that you are still willing to buy mine, too."

"Please, wait for me a minute," Leemu said quickly and rushed into her house. Coming back, she told Suah, "Here are some old clothes along with these empty bags for you. Instead of the amount you are charging, I'm giving you fifty dollars for the two bags. The change will be for my daughter's friend to buy some exercise books for her school."

Suah said, "She doesn't go to school. Anyway, thank you so much for everything. I pray that the Lord of all the heavens will continue to bless you and your family."

"Thank you so much for that," Leemu said. "Every little blessing brings more blessings. You made me think about my paternal grandmother. She used to bless me the same way."

Leemu left the bags of charcoal and came closer to Suah. "By the way, are you a Christian?"

"Uhm, well…something like that."

"I hope I am not embarrassing you?"

"No, it is not actually that. I have just experienced a slow pace of the tongue. I was actually baptized by a colonial missionary into a denomination most people don't really know about it."

"And which one is that?"

"Have you ever heard the words 'Sabbath Church'?"

"Yes! But, I'm not surprised. By the time I saw you, I knew you were a believer. If I can remember anything about that denomination, I won't forget the health message it promulgates. I once learned that they are the longest lifespan Christians or people because of their vegetarian diet. I like vegetarian diets, no eating pork, crab, catfish, unclean or junk food, and things, even though I don't eat it everyday. I try sometimes to follow their diet as a medical practitioner."

The two ladies looked at one another and affectionately hugged. Appearing so free, they talked with one another as if they were two biological sisters or if they had known one another for a long time.

"So, my friend, you are free to bring some more charcoal any time," Leemu offered Suah, without knowing that she was bridging a life-long friendship, not only with Suah and Latto, but with the entire village of Payeta.

"I'm happy that we have opened a hand of friendship. We are becoming one family; I can promise you that I will make myself available to you for any local work you want to be done, either here or in my village." Suah shook hands with Leemu once again and said, "Please let me go and to prepare for my working group that is coming to my farm this Monday."

Chapter 3

Once the sale was completed between Suah and Leemu, the sun had already gone behind the trees, showing that the day was gone. As a farmer, Suah became impatient. She wanted to complete her itinerary before sunset. From the porch, she faced the hallway and called Latto in order for them to go home, since all their goods had been bought.

Latto was nowhere to be found. Paying no attention to anything else, only eager to complete her business to go through with Leemu, Suah did not know where Latto might have gone without her permission.

By the time they entered the porch, while Suah was bargaining with Leemu, Latto had gone into the house. She began to play with her compassionate friend, Manu. She had shown Latto all her dolls, her clothes, uniforms, and other school materials. She turned on the television set and played some already recorded cartoon programs.

Latto was astonished to see those animated images on the television screen, singing and dancing like real human beings, she absorbed herself into this life as if she hadn't come on a business trip. Manu explained the meaning of every scene and the name of each actor to Latto.

As Latto strode around the Mediterranean furniture, she talked to herself, "See how Manu and her family are blessed!" She felt so disappointed when she saw, hanging on the wall her friend's family's portraits and said, "I wish my parents could read and write, too. See how honorable this family appears."

Latto once learned that many elite people requested her father, Yallon, to stay with them to go to school, but he refused. Yallon had vowed to take care of his widowed mother, Sianniah and his two younger brothers, Torkolon and Nuwoe. The next thing Yallon did was to marry the fifteen-year-old girl, Suah, from a distant land when he too had just turned twenty. After their marriage, Yallon left his widowed mother with her children in their village, Kpanshue. He settled with his wife in Payeta.

By the end of sixteen years of marriage, Latto's parents already had four children; constantly quarreling and still unprepared to provide all their basic needs, one of which was a formal western education.

In fact, since Yallon and his family along with his in-laws lived together under one roof, he had dual responsibilities. He cared for Jesse and Neh Korto, Suah's parents, along with some of their extended family members. Jesse had lost his left eye when he was cutting palm thatches to build a shelter for the rice they had harvested, just eight years after Suah and Yallon's wedding. Due to the unavailability of curable modern medical treatments in Payeta, Jesse died from that excruciating pain a few years later.

Latto, who had been ignoring her mother's call, finally informed Manu, "I have to go. My mother has been calling for me so we can go back home. It was a nice time being with you, my friend. One day, I will see you whenever we come to sell again."

"I heard all of that," Manu answered, feeling reluctant to grant her friend permission to leave her.

Both of them stood speechless, looking at one another in sorrow, praying for some sort of reverse decision from either of their parents. Then, they eventually hugged and told one another farewell. She handed Latto one of her dolls and a dress as her eyes watered but she controlled her emotions.

Feeling so lonely, Manu turned once again and told Latto, "Ah! Can you stay with me, please?"

"How long will it take? You know my mother is calling me?"

"For some weeks or forever." Manu answered.

"How can I do that? Inasmuch as I would like to, I can't do it for now."

"Why not? Please do it my friend. I don't have a sister. I want you to be my sister. I will talk with my mother. I know it won't be any problem for her to allow you to stay with us."

Latto pretended to answer her friend unwillingly. "That's a good idea, but my mother won't agree to that for now."

"Why she won't be happy that someone wants to send you to school? Do you know how many people usually come to my parents to beg for this opportunity?"

"I may not know the number, but I believe there are many. If I would go to my mother and cry about this, she would still not do it. You know mothers always love their children and they don't want them to be away from them," said Latto. "Do you know how many times I have tried to convince my mother to let me go to school?"

"I do not want you to lose this opportunity, which may not come to you in the same way," Manu said. "You will live to regret passing on this opportunity, my friend. You must be the woman for your family tomorrow, only when you get yourself educated."

"I know this," Latto said as she pretended to let herself through the doorway to go to the porch where her mother was seated with Leemu.

Then, Manu quickly rushed and held the doorframe at both sides, blocking Latto any free passage. She said, "Why must you be difficult, throwing the blame on your mother? You see Numeh. He is the only brother I have. My parents would appreciate if you would stay with us. I know they would accept you as my sister. Several times, I have heard them discuss about finding a submissive girl-child to be their second daughter. In fact, my parents will send you to school, since you told me that your desire is to be educated."

"Ah, Manu, I know you are trying your best for me to stay. My mother has a lot of things going on. She has suffered a lot. She could have had seven children by now. Her first children who were twins died at their births, while our older brother, Dahn, died from a certain lump in his stomach. My surviving two sisters, Wianneh and Zonpu along with our brother, Jucuma, do not help my mother with any of the domestic works. Understanding between my mother and my father is not that cordial. Most villagers continue to make mockery about her family life. Since I am the only person who always tries to help her, she does not want to lose me. She doesn't like for me to go anywhere without her. I know it is a difficult matter. If you are serious about it, please go and tell your mother to ask my mother about it."

"I will! Leave the rest to me," Manu happily said.

Latto and Manu ran to the porch where their mothers were seated.

When Latto's mother saw them, running toward them, she said, "Latto, why are you running all over in the people's house, without taking into consideration that you have come to sell?"

"That doesn't matter, Ma'am. Children are always quick to find friends. They are also the medium of connecting families," Leemu said, trying to clear out the embarrassing feeling from Suah.

Manu anxiously looked on and said, "Mommy, please tell Latto's mother to let her stay with us. I want her to be my sister!" She hauled her mother by her dress in an attempt to convince her to accept her request.

"Please Manu, you are full of troubles. Please don't bother the people. They have things to do."

"Mommy, I have not seen a friend so nice like Latto. Please let her spend the break with us."

Applying her motherly wit in order to convince her daughter, Leemu said, "Please wait when they come the next time, then you will ask your friend to stay."

"No, Mommy!" Manu insisted, "I want her to stay with us today. Please Mommy?"

Manu dropped on the ground and began to cry as Latto and her mother stood by to watch the proceedings with a prayerful heart that the little girl's mother should consider her appeal.

"Get up," Leemu commanded. "Why must you roll on the ground like a two-year-old child? You need to learn how to make your point instead of crying."

Manu quickly stood up and wiped her face. She went and stood with Latto as they both looked at their mothers for consideration.

Leemu stood up for a while and later went closer to Suah and said, "Please permit me to ask you for a favor."

"Sure," said Suah.

"My daughter's school has closed. She will be on her vacation for two long weeks. My husband and I will always be in and out of the home during this period. My daughter doesn't have a sister to play with.

"So, Ma'am, would it be possible for you to allow your daughter to spend the break with us? I know you may feel uncomfortable about such a request. You haven't built enough confidence in me. We have just met today. But that's how most lasting friendships can start. We are all one people. You and I speak the same Kpelle language from the same district. If we allow some elderly people to describe us, we would be surprised to know that we are somehow related. I know the matter concerning children is delicate for women to handle without the presence of their husbands in Leewah. We will not complete every discussion today, but please let her spend the two weeks with us. This is all I am asking for."

With a comfortable smile, Suah answered Leemu. "Ma'am, how can I say no to such a wonderful humanitarian gesture from such a nice person like you? A child doesn't belong to one person. A child belongs to the community. It's only now that the care for children has become the responsibility of their parents only."

But Leemu said, "even though we do live in the world where every man is afraid of his own shadow, any good family member can live like a humanitarian person. Having a hand in raising other people's children mattered to the people who brought us up. It's our responsibility to do the same thing to anyone we see in need. That's our gospel."

"Not everybody does it in this confused world," Suah argued. "If a pigeon that is protective of its chicks for any circumstance should allow another bird to care for its young, then it should be the loving dove, but not the carnivorous hawk. During the few hours I have spent with you, I have known that you are a good person. Also, I have no fear leaving my daughter with you, because we both have the same indigenous background. If Latto agrees to stay, I will tell her father and the rest of the kinsmen when I reach home."

Upon hearing Suah's response, Latto shouted, "I agree!"

Latto and Manu thanked their mothers as they pulled on one another and ran back into the house to continue their play.

Leemu looked behind the children with satisfaction and said, "If every man were like children, I don't think there would be problems in this world. They are quick to make up for anything."

Suah said, "That is why those who plan to harm children are agents of the devil."

Both women stood for a while with still-eyes, looking into one another face, and then they laughed.

Suah requested once again, "Well! Please let me go."

"Okay, when you are coming after the two weeks please bring some more bags of charcoal for us to buy. Your daughter will be fine with us. Don't worry about her. Please extend our regards to your husband and the other children."

Hurriedly, Suah wrapped up the few things she bought along with the empty bags and the few pieces of clothing Leemu gave her.

Before leaving, she offered all of them a good-bye as she hugged Latto and the rest.

When Suah had traveled mid-way home, she stopped at the stream pouring from a heap in the forest. She picked up some green leaves and folded them like a cup; she went down to the stream to drink some of the cold water with it. Thereafter, she inhaled some of the fresh air and her mind became so clouded about her daughter's future. She said, "Latto is not experienced like my other children, especially Wianneh, her bigger sister. Even though Wianneh and her husband, Nah-Jon along with my other children solely depend on me for everything, they are mature. Latto is not, but she is helpful to me. Who will accompany me? Who will chat with me like Latto? Who will go with me to the farm and who will go with me anywhere I want to go?"

She said, "Once a child tastes the educated man's water, it is always difficult for that child to come back home. Since, Latto will spend a couple of days in this home, tasting their way of living, she will be changed. I am worried that my daughter is on her way to be separated from me forever." She prayed for the best.

She remembered that during the colonial days, when an elite person discovered that a child was serviceable, they never allowed the child to go back home. "Even though the child might have suffered in coping with the living standard of the pioneer, that child's life was always changed for the best."

Before she could continue her journey, she hoped, "If this family will hold on to my baby let them be nice to her. Let them send Latto to school so that a better life will come through her to erase my shame tomorrow."

Upon reaching Payeta, Suah met her husband in a hammock as his colleagues brought him home. The entire village became tense. A village with a fewer number of residence, losing Yallon could mean an unbearable loss even to the entire region. No one could easily take his place of being humorous and cooperative, especially when he was not under the influence of any high beverage; he was the darling among his friends in the village. The women and the children left the town center, crying and wondering what might have gone wrong with Yallon. Chief Dokpa Jao of the village had been informed. Upon his arrival, and looking at the condition of Yallon, he immediately considered the case as a civil one, which meant someone must be punished, because the norms of the region did not tolerate the act involving the loss of someone's life. He had dispatched the village's messenger to call the most important members of his family, including his brothers, Torkolon and Nuwoe along with his wife, Suah. Even, his senior brother-in-law, Myron, had been informed.

Nah-Botto, the Chief Zoë, came in, checked on Yallon thoroughly and inquired from the people who had worked with him on that day. From his findings, it was discovered that Yallon and Qualilon had challenged one another with liquors after they had finished, clearing the bush from Sulonteh's new farm. They wanted to show their onlookers who could drink more liquor. As their onlookers flattered them, they mixed in bitter roots palm wine and cane juice. After drinking the larger quantity of the liquors and declared the winner of the competition, Yallon was in the highest degree of a drunken stupor with foams of saliva running from his mouth. When they opened his eyes, they could see all the white areas behind both eyes, which had turned pale and seemingly dead. He hardly moved any of his limbs.

Many arrests had been made, including Yallon's main challenger, Qualilon along with Jembah, the head of the male working group.

Fromo Vokie, one of the leading herbalists in the area, prepared a spicy, fermented fluid from several tropical leaves and poured it into his nostrils and mouth for several hours. Later, Yallon began to sneeze, vomit and opened his eyes feebly.

Suah quickly prepared hot bathing water and washed the mess from her husband. After several hours of slumbering, Yallon was somehow sobered from the liquors. Suah offered him a palatable dish with rice and hot pepper soup.

As Yallon was eating, he shouted, "Latto come and eat with me!" The call caught the attention of his two brothers and other family members who were still around, making sure that nothing was seriously wrong with Yallon. They began to ask Suah for the whereabouts of Latto.

Since all the important family members were present, Suah informed them that the Kiamu family, the medical practitioners of the nearby teaching hospital, who seemed to be nice people, had asked that Latto spend two weeks with them. She showed them the gifts Leemu gave her and how things went on between them.

As other family members somehow accepted the revelation from Suah, Torkolon became upset and warned, "Suah make sure nothing goes wrong with our daughter. I do not think you were right to have left our child there without our consent. You are not a man to make decisions without our consent."

Nuwoe, who had earlier threatened to deal with Qualilon if Yallon did not survive; this time, came in to calm his brother and other family members who seemed unhappy. He said, "As husbands or men, we have the right to vet every issue that confronts our family, but we cannot vex the situation. In other words, we must be parts of the solutions, but not to add to the problem that comes to our family."

He made the people understand that opportunity sometimes comes to people unexpectedly. "I beg that we respect Suah and her marriage. She is a good wife, trying her best to see to it that her family is fed and cared for. I do not think she would plan to throw Latto into the mouths of wolves. Let's respect the decision she has made, and let's wait for the result," he advised.

Chapter 4

It was an interesting night for Latto; she had never slept somewhere without her mother. Continuing to watch television, sleeping on a sponge mattress, under an electric light, she was excited at this time to spend a couple of days with her newly found people who were willing to send her to school.

Latto along with Leemu and Manu had been waiting for Dr. Kiamu that evening. The family was getting concerned, as the two extra hours he could have spent before coming home that night had passed.

As the administrator of the only hospital and school of nursing in the region, Dr. Kiamu had been in a meeting with some representatives from the hospital's Board of Trustees.

The Board of Trustees had finally decided to extend the services of the hospital into a mini-clinic network in fifty major villages in the Central Province. They were going to train people from each of the targeted villages as village health workers to start a revolving drug fund project. As the donors and the facilitators planned it, if the pilot stage of the project was properly maintained, it would eventually spread to all regions of Leewah.

The project, which seemed to be one of the best health care delivery systems, was intended to treat every villager at a minimum cost. At least ten percent payment was charged to augment the cost of the drugs and to help with the expense of the system.

As Manu looked on the road, she said, "There comes Daddy," rejoicing as she ran to the Land Rover Jeep, rolling down the driveway of the house. "I have some good news for you, Daddy." Manu didn't mind that there was an additional passenger in the vehicle with her father. She continued to rush on telling her father her news.

"Let me open the door before I wound you," said Dr. Kiamu to his daughter.

After seeing Manu, wishing to tell her father about her, Latto's heart pondered and she asked, "Why must she be the first person to tell her father about me? Why can't she wait for her mother to do so?

"I fear, when Manu says anything about me to her father in the public, he might react negatively. I know that most men are critical when it comes to making decisions about another person's child. I wish her mother would be the first person to tell her husband about me when they are in bed."

When Dr. Kiamu finally opened the car's door and came out, Manu showed him Latto, her friend.

"She came with her Mom to sell charcoal, and I told her to stay with us. She is a nice friend; we have played the whole day," Manu said.

As Latto watched, Manu's father just nodded, unwilling to discuss anything about another person's child in haste, especially while there was a guest for dinner.

His wife also came and kissed him by the car. She welcomed the guest, who stood by the car next to Dr. Kiamu.

She turned to her husband, "Here we are again!"

"What?" Dr. Kiamu asked.

"Your daughter," she answered, avoiding any blame for her action.

"What did she do?" asked Dr. Kiamu as he looked firmly into the eyes of his wife, expecting no surprise.

"She turned our home into another studio show today."

"What is a studio show?"

"A lady and her daughter came to sell charcoal today. When Manu saw them, she cried that the lady's daughter should spend Easter vacation with us."

"No problem, honey. It is her choice. It's a nice thing for children to open up to their peers. We can't limit our children to what we want all the time.

"Anyway, we will discuss that, but please meet Dr. Joel Errol Brokmann. He is a member of our Board of Trustees."

Leemu welcomed Dr. Brokmann as they shook hands once again before they proceeded to the living room.

Looking at the various kinds of African vegetables flourishing around the house, Dr. Brokmann made a quick stop. Dr. Kiamu joined him as he began to name each vegetable one by one. Leemu rushed into the kitchen to make sure that everything was okay for dinner.

Later, Dr. Kiamu entered the living room and sat on a low bench to take off his shoes. Latto stood behind Manu to peek at him, wondering who Dr. Kiamu actually was.

Manu observed that Latto had been looking at her father since he came from work. She said, "Latto, don't worry about him. He is a good father. As long as I can remember, my dad hasn't been violent to any child. He always chats with me even if I have gone contrary to his expectations."

"That is good." Latto said with a surprise, "In the culture that I know, this is not a usual thing for our fathers. No child does nonsense. They can quickly take the hell out of him or her. You must be a good child, Manu. Maybe your father had learned that kind of lifestyle from some of the many places he had traveled before."

"Maybe, he's just a good father, Latto. Many people travel and they don't put into use what they had learned abroad.

"I know traveling has nothing to do with showing good ways to other people.

"My Daddy is a down-to-earth father. He wrestles with me like we are equals. He is the best friend I have for now. Sometimes, I freely lay myself in his chest until I sleep. I love doing that, especially when I'm upset. He cradles me as if I was a few-days-old child. That's the way a loving father does with his children without abusing their rights."

Latto listened to Manu with satisfaction. She prayed that the Lord should make it possible for her to stay with these people and enjoy some of the good life they were living. She thought, "How long will it take me to know that these people are good people? I have already seen that they are good people by the way they talk with me and welcome strangers. They too will soon get to know who I'm in a short time. When I love them, do any job perfectly and on time before they tell me, by this way I know they will also love me."

Chapter 5

Leemu came through the doorway and waved, calling to her husband and Dr. Brokmann that dinner was ready. As the two men continued to talk and to look at the vegetables, they delayed coming as quick as Leemu wanted them to do. She went and took her husband by the right hand, while the guest followed them as they walked to the dining table.

Latto had observed how Leemu had set up everything at the dining table. She placed a chair before the table, a set of cutlery, and a napkin. Each food item was placed in a separate big bowl along with a bottle of juice by the side.

"This is the first time I'm going to eat with this kind of finger-like spoon, and a knife at a table," Latto laughed as she wondered how to use them. "In fact, how do you eat with knives? Knives are good for cutting vegetables and meats. Eating with knives at a dining table, I am not used to that. How will a knife hold the food like human fingers? This is a murky idea, and it's also funny."

As it seemed to be silly, Latto said, "In the village, we usually place the food in our mouths with our fingers instead of knives. As we eat together from one bowl, the children eat without messing in the food or chewing with their mouths open. The children lick on the bones or eat the heads of the animals, while the elderly people eat the fleshy parts of the animals. When the children are eating with older people, they hold on to the bowl that contains the food with their left hands to prevent it from sliding under their hands. No child is the first to say he or she is full or to leave while the older people are still eating. It is the child's responsibility to wait upon the elders to eat to their satisfaction, and leave the bowl with him or her. If the child is the first to leave the area, who will clean up the place and wash the dishes? When the children have done the right thing, the older people would know that their parents and the community have trained them to be respectful."

When Latto saw the spaghetti, which Leemu had prepared with a tomato sauce, she said, "This kind of foodstuff looks like a worm," she chuckled. She quickly went closer to Manu at the other end of the table and whispered in a way that their parents and the guest wouldn't notice what they were discussing. "Manu, what do you call this kind of stuff, that long stuff over there?"

"Oh, you mean this?"

"Yes!"

"It is called spaghetti," answered Manu shortly.

"I haven't seen it before, how do you eat it."

Manu described the spaghetti as one of the food items she loves. She joked, "If a person were looking for a house rogue, I would be the one if I was left alone around prepared spaghetti." She encouraged Latto to take some of it.

Without a rush, Latto watched everyone as they picked up a set of cutlery. They followed one another as they mounded their plates with as much food as they could finish.

As Latto observed them, she followed their patterns; and said to herself, "I should be careful to take what I think I can eat." She didn't want to disgrace herself, especially with the kind of food she had not eaten before.

She reminded herself, "This time, I'm eating flesh at a dining table. I can't believe myself living like chief Jao in our village."

After the dinner, Leemu and her husband along with their guest went to the living room.

As the guest looked at the couple, he began to talk, "We adopted a boy last year. He is so cute and submissive. I wish my wife and I had adopted him many years ago. We have been living without a child since our marriage three years ago. We had finally decided that it was better to adopt a child. We are happy as it was the nicest idea that we ever had."

"It is good to have a child," said Dr. Kiamu, unwilling to engage in such a discussion while Latto was also visiting them. In fact, he didn't want to discuss family business with a guest whom they had just met. But the guest didn't notice the mood of Dr. Kiamu was in.

He continued with the same topic. "Many men and women who are successful today were either once orphans or adopted by somebody. A good example was Mark. Counselor Garrison adopted Mark from a remote village. Mark had been looking for such an opportunity since the deaths of his parents. He was nearly seventeen years by the time he was adopted. He usually woke up by the crows of the chickens to do his house work, filling drums with water from a nearby creek.

"When the Garrisons died, Mark inherited their wealth as their direct heir. He is a renowned educator in my area today."

"That's so true, Sir," said Leemu, pretending to be little fascinated by his story. "Just as it was in the days of Mark, so it is today. There are good children, too."

"Is this your first time visiting this region?" Dr. Kiamu interrupted the conversation to change the direction.

"Yes," Dr. Brokmann said. "As a board member, I have traveled to many parts of the world where we have hospitals and clinics. I was eager to make this trip so that I could see our hospital and school in Leewah."

From the children's bedroom, Latto had been listening to the conversation while she pretended to be playing with Manu and Numeh.

The story impressed her. It introduced many lessons into her mind. Like she had always done when a good storyteller told them stories in the village, she had listened and picked up the moral lesson from the story.

Latto said, "If Mark could endure every circumstance to be an important person, I can do it even better than he did. My mother has always told me, 'a squirrel will never dig a hole without a bloody nose. It takes a feather and a stick at a time for the bird to build its nest. Every successful man must strive for something before he can achieve it. There is no success without a struggle. There is no easy way in life. If at first you tried and you did not succeed, don't quit. You must continue to try, one day you will succeed.'

"Now, it is my time to do the same thing. I must strive hard. I must suffer for this wealthy cause for tomorrow.

"In fact, I have just spent less than twelve hours in this home. I think I have done some good work, which has already motivated my newly found family to like me. I do not think people usually like children because they are beautifully dressed. Children are loved best by the way they behave."

When it was devotion time, Latto watched Manu and Numeh sing along with their parents beautifully. She was so amazed by the way the devotion was conducted. She said, "I wish I could sing like these children. They aren't looking in the hymnal as they sing. They have learned these songs over and over since they were born. I'm also good at singing our traditional songs. If I stay with them for a longer time, I would memorize these songs and be able to sing like everyone else."

After the devotion, the children went to bed. Numeh asked Manu to offer Latto some pajamas for the night.

"What's a pajama?" Latto asked as she went and stood by Manu, changing into her nightgown.

"They are clothes! You wear them for the night," Manu replied. "This is one of them I'm wearing.

"Please wear this set and get yourself ready for bed."

"Why do you want me to wear these new clean clothes, when I'm going to sleep?" Latto asked.

"They will help you to enjoy your sleep. My mother usually tells us that fresh air at night makes children grow healthy. She even advises that we should not wear tight clothes. They embarrass people in many ways."

While changing her dress, Latto showed Manu and Numeh, "You see this dress. It was Uncle Myron, my mother's older brother, who bought it for me two Christmas seasons ago. I usually wear it when I'm going to an important occasion with my mother."

Numeh asked, "It seems like you love to wear it, right?"

"Not exactly that. That's the only dress I have," Latto replied. "Why shouldn't I love it? You can only carry on the love and hate game when you have more to choose from. A man would only refuse to eat fermented food when he knows where to get the new one from. My mother has always told me that monkeys do not like pepper, but when they are hungry, they usually eat it without minding the hotness."

Numeh was shocked by the great surprise and stared at Latto. He couldn't believe that in this world where people have more clothes than they usually wear, there would be a person in dire need for some and she can't get them.

As Latto sat in the next bed, looking sadly at Manu and Numeh, she said, "It's not a nice thing to live on an island teeming with poverty. It teaches you how to be very careful with the little resource you have."

"You are right! Don't worry. I'm going to give you some of my dresses before you go to the village." Manu promised. "By the way, who says you are going to that village? You have come from the hell, why do you want to go back there again? You don't really want to do that!"

"No, Manu. I will make Daddy and Mommy buy Latto some new clothes. They always do that for strangers," Numeh assured.

Latto smiled as she stood up to hang her only dress on the rack in the closet. She couldn't say anything anymore. She didn't want to belittle her mother who had always done the best for her family, too.

Uncle Myron once told Latto that the family's legacy depends on the way each member defends the reputation of that family. He told her that other people would talk about how each member conducts his or her business, especially in the public.

Latto turned herself into a silent lamb and continued to listen to Manu and Numeh, discussing one thing or the other until sleep took each of them along the path to little death.

Chapter 6

Latto had many nightmares during that night about the new life she was entering into. Above all, she had been dreaming about how she would impress her newly found family to fully accept her like the other children.

She imagined how her villagers would think about her after benefiting from a better life with the Kiamu family. She imagined her many blessings beyond the Kiamus' home on the hospital compound. She imagined how she would be counted among educated people around the world. She imagined how she would be the source to bring the white man's civilization of education, farm-to-market roads, electricity, pipe-borne water and a clinic to Payeta.

She had built up her plan in her mind to be brutally honest in all that she would do as the way to impress her newly found family.

A jingle from the wall clock in the living room woke her up. She was the first person to wake up that Saturday morning.

Latto knelt by her bed's side while Manu and Numeh were still asleep. She chanted some traditional rhymes to her ancestors and to her host family for the hospitality she had received so far.

Without any delay, after the chanting, she went into the kitchen and washed the dishes, swept the house, and prepared some hot water for her newly found parents' bath.

Leemu, who had just woken up, emerged from her bedroom and saw that the morning work had been done. She asked, "Yonkor, are you here?"

Yonkor was not there to respond. No one else answered her.

"I wonder who might have done them, when Yonkor isn't yet around?" she talked to herself.

As Leemu was standing by the pantry, finding something for breakfast, she spotted Latto coming from the living room area.

She greeted her and asked, "How well did you sleep?"

"Fine, Mommy."

"Who did all these jobs around here?"

Going closer to the coal-pot to make sure that the fire was blazing well, Latto answered Leemu, "I did, Mommy."

"Hmm, how old are you?"

"Eleven!"

"Look, we have a cook. She had been on a little break due to some troubles in her family. She was supposed to be here this morning. She is responsible to do these jobs. We pay her with some good money for the housekeeping. Next time, don't bother to do that, okay? Anyway, thank you so much."

"Mommy, I'm a handy person in my parents' home. My mother has taught me all the domestic jobs a woman is believed to do. I'm her last child. She made me know these things for my future. Please Ma'am, don't stop me from doing anything while I'm here.

"I can't eat and put the dishes down for someone else to wash them for me. I would feel guilty and embarrassed that I'm not a good child. I am used to cutting down hard trees and gathering them to burn them as charcoal. I traveled many miles to sell it so my mother could underwrite the cost of our farming, our meals, our clothes, and to maintain our name in society. Doing these little domestic jobs wouldn't be any problem for me."

Trying to overcome surprise she watched Latto, talking like a mature housewife; Leemu cleared out her throat as she replied to her, "Oh no honey, you are a good child."

After talking with Latto, Leemu went to her husband in their bedroom and said, "Daddy, you will not believe it. We have a wonderful child, visiting us."

"Why do you say that?" her husband asked.

"She has done all the morning jobs," she stated.

"But sweet, you are talking like you haven't slept in any village. That is what the girl-children learn when they are growing up. Their parents and the community teach them moral values.

"You will be surprised to know that Latto can cook, wash, and do many other domestic jobs. All we have to do is to increase our love for her as a motivating factor for her to enjoy her stay with us," he explained.

"It's easy for any obedient child to adapt to any situation. Good children always pave the way for people to like them. If she continues, we will consider her like a child who just needs some help," Leemu promised.

"What child like Latto wouldn't like any help?" Dr. Kiamu asked.

"There are many children around here who need some help and they can't get it. What's about the ones in the rural areas?" she asked

"Most of the ones in the urban areas have bad behavior is their main problem," Dr. Kiamu revealed.

While they were still talking, Manu opened their bedroom door and greeted them.

Leemu commanded, "Let's go to the Living room and join Latto for the devotion."

"So, now you have a friend?" asked Dr. Kiamu.

"Yeah," Manu replied with a smile. "Not a friend, but a sister."

"Ah, I understand my mother's name's sake…

"I know you didn't sleep very much last night."

"Somehow, Daddy."

"I was still hearing you until I fell asleep."

"No Daddy, we went to sleep early enough so that we could wake up to do our morning jobs. In fact, Latto woke up early and did everything."

"Well, let us straighten out a few things. We are not going to work today. You know that your school is already closed for the Easter break," Dr. Kiamu said.

"Yeah," Manu answered.

"We may go out to do some shopping after devotion," he said.

Meanwhile, as the family was conducting the devotion, the cook, Yonkor, sneaked into the kitchen. She placed her right palm on to her chest, appearing somehow frightened for coming late due to the funeral services she had attended for two of her hometown men who had died from eating a poisonous snake.

Yonkor looked around and said, "I wonder who might have done all my work this early morning." Feeling that she was going to lose her job by coming to work late, she went on, "If my boss could do the entire morning job, I have already fired myself." As a widow, she wondered if she lost this job how she could continue to support her child in school.

Yonkor was surprised to see Latto, sitting with the family as she looked through the service window between the kitchen and the living room.

"I'm sure it is that little girl who has done all this work," said Yonkor.

After the devotion, Latto went with her family to Lewisville for shopping.

Dr. Kiamu always made his children to feel good whenever they were shopping. This time, he said, "Children, get what you have put on the shopping list and do not pick up what you do not need."

"Daddy, you know your children like everything. You will make Manu want to buy the whole store, honey," Leemu said.

"I will evaluate what all they pick out before I pay for it."

Even Latto appearing timid, still picked up the pair of sandals she had always wished for, colorful ones.

"Do you like them?" Manu asked.

"Sure!"

Latto happily said, "I'm so excited about wearing this pair of sandals. I have longed for some throughout the years, but my mother couldn't afford them. My father does not look for the means to buy things for us."

"Well, you have the chance now. You should pick out a dress, too. Don't be shy. That's what my parents do for us. They won't mind doing the same thing for you. You are not a stranger; but one of their children now," Manu encouraged Latto.

"You plan to make me look like one of the city girls," asked Latto as she picked up a stripy blue and white dress; while Manu added a head tie and a belt to it.

"For sure, you need to be cute, Latto."

Chapter 7

It was another beautiful evening. Latto and her family walked into the hall where the hospital had a banquet for the delegates. The hospital had called all the chiefs from the fifty earmarked villages where they planned to undertake the mini-clinic network project for the official launching that night.

Like most of the doctors, nurses, and other workers of the hospital, Dr. Kiamu and his family along with Latto attended the program. Latto wore her new dress and the pair of sandals. She was very mindful about walking in the new sandals for the first time. Falling in the midst of the crowd could bring some sort of disgrace, not only to her, but to anybody who was connected to her. She walked humbly, sometimes like she was hopping with a wounded leg.

Before leaving the house, Manu had called Latto to the side and advised her. "When I was much younger, my parents told me one thing, which I want to give to you Latto. They advised me,

> Before going to any program, you must eat enough food at home and also make sure to use the restroom at home. If you have a stomach ache, which would make you to go to the restroom more frequently; it would be better for you to remain at home to avoid further embarrassment.
>
> While getting ready to go out, look at yourself in a mirror and make sure that you look neat. When you enter the hall

where the program is held, you should walk slowly, while you go to the area that is provided for people like you. Before sitting, lift up the chair and pull it towards you. Find a space between the chair and the table to sit freely without detracting others' attention. If you would ever sneeze, cough or clean your nose, bend your head and do it in your arm or in a handkerchief, and wipe your face thoroughly before lifting up your head. Sometimes, chewing a spicy sweet or gum keeps the mouth watery, fresh, and odorless.

Watch others. Whatever they are doing, like clapping hands, do the same thing. You must watch and listen keenly during the program that is how people get some common sense.

"At first, I thought it was an embarrassing comment. Over the years, I have found out that it has been useful to me.

"I thought it was useful to pass it over to you, Latto. I hope I am not appearing bossy to you."

"Oh no, my sister!" Latto said. "From the time I got to know myself, my mother has been teaching me most of these etiquettes. I'm happy that you have given me another version of them.

"No piece of advice is nonsense. 'Only the fool despises wisdom.' It's always better to listen to all kinds of ideas and it's left up to you to take the best ones from among them.

"My mother always says, 'you must hear quick, quick, but you must not talk quick, quick.'"

At the program, Latto had looked everywhere her eye sight could reach. She admired the decorations, the glamorous flowers, the beautiful linens on the tables and the radiant light everywhere. "I can smell the sweet deodorant and perfume the people are wearing. Melodious music is heard from every corner of the hall.

I'm amazed. I have always wished to attend one of the closing programs of this nursing school," she said.

Then, Manu replied, "Latto you are just starting. There will be many programs like this held around here. You will be tired of watching them in your life."

The boring life in the village could not make Latto miss being there. She wondered, "What is so fascinating about the village? Good people like the ones we see around here aren't there to talk with us, share their experiences with us. We don't know what the future holds for us. We live in the vacuum of doubts like a baboon sleeping under a bunch of ripe bananas unaware.

"The one thing we know is to go to the farm everyday and at the end to marry early and begin to have a bunch of children whom we are unable to prepare for the future."

"Especially when there is no school to keep you busy," Manu supported.

"Yeah! That is the worst part of it," Numeh said.

"None of my female relatives has ever been to school. Only my cousin Kelikow, Uncle Jimmy's son has done that. He had even traveled to an unknown white man's land to learn more last year," Latto revealed. "Like my two big sisters, they always feel embarrassed whenever they see educated people around them or accompany my mother to a program. My mother always complained about them. She had not found out why they always refused to do so."

"That is sad. It happens to anybody who does not know certain things," said Manu. "I mean, if you are not educated, you somehow feel inferior to come around the educated ones. In fact, you gain the courage to come around them, you may do the harder and manual work than the one they would do."

"The world needs educated young men and women," Numeh added.

"I wish your parents could have learned their lesson from their past. They could have been willing to find means in their little weak ways to educate you and your siblings. They didn't have to be rich or educated to sacrifice their lives for you," said Manu. "There are many illiterate people who are educating their children."

"That's so true. I pray that one day I will have the opportunity to go to school to help my people someday," Latto explained.

"Latto, my mommy always says, 'The Lord will provide.' Just trust in the Lord. You will have the opportunity to get your education, there's no question about that."

During the first two weeks of her stay, Latto had impressed her newly found family with her morality. Even the people who usually visited the home admired the young village girl, and they began to ask whether they could adopt her.

One day, Dr. Kiamu informed his wife that a child like Latto needed some help. They had been sitting under the mango tree in their back yard. He knew that his wife was aware of the child's problem. He believed that if a chance was given to the child, she would have agreed.

Leemu asked her husband, "What kind of help are you talking about?"

"What help is better than adopting and educating a child?" he responded. "I think it would be better for us to adopt her as our second girl child. Bearing another child when we are already waxed should not be our thinking for now."

"Well, honey, you aren't God. I know God can do any good thing for anybody at anytime. What we have to do is to always look up to the Lord," Leemu rebuked her husband.

"Yes, it is a good thing that God is always telling us what to do," Dr. Kiamu agreed.

"Adoption is a good idea. I never took it seriously when we first discussed it that night."

"Why?"

"I wanted to make sure that we aren't going in for raising a lion."

"What do you mean by that?"

"I don't want us to raise a child that will bring us more trouble than happiness. Furthermore, I wanted you to say it for the second time for me to know that we actually need another child."

"Which child will not be troublesome? Every human being performs a certain bad behavior at times. We should pray for the obedient and hard-working one. I was serious that night as serious as I am today," said Dr. Kiamu. "How do you want me to appear before you know that I am serious?"

"Well, I don't want a child who will only spend a few days with us and go back to her people. I want us to adopt a child we will love with all our hearts like the other children."

Being impressed by the interest Latto had shown as a good child, Dr. Kiamu said to his wife, "I don't think this child will fail us. Let's go in for her."

"Anyway, let us wait for her mother to come in two weeks' time," she replied.

Chapter 8

Learning from all that had transpired, Dr. Kiamu believed that the love of parents surpasses every other love. He knew that mothers are the earthly gods for their children. He argued that though mothers are not divine beings, if they do not permit a child to be born, such a child would not be born at the right time.

Dr. Kiamu believed that every human being was born by a mother. He warned that no one should challenge to stop that way in life, and people of every walk of life need to understand and respect mothers for their sacrifices they render for their children.

Dr. Kiamu, who was also a pediatric instructor of the nursing school, recalled the wonderful love he had received from his biological parents as well as those who adopted him. He was less than eight years old when he was adopted by a God-fearing family, an elite family, who sponsored him to the level of education he wanted. He promised himself that it was a time to do a similar thing for any child in need.

He had seen how Suah cared for her family as one of the strong mothers of those days in Leewah.

"Why do you say that?" asked Leemu.

"I don't have to go to the Holy Land to be a prophet before I can know what is right or wrong. You can see the way Suah presents herself, showing that she really loves Latto and the other children. She has given her a sound moral education," said Dr. Kiamu.

"It won't be an easy task for anybody to extract Latto from her mother," Leemu replied.

"You think so? Once someone is nice to a child, that child will be persuaded by the kindness to follow that person," Dr. Kiamu argued.

"Yeah! It's also said that children usually do well with their biological parents, but on a larger spectrum, they belong to the society. Within the society, there are social institutions or humanitarian people who act as surrogates to children whose parents are unable to provide their basic needs love and care.

"Most surrogate parents provide joy to disadvantaged children as if they were still with their biological parents. That is the way we got our education through good and concerned people," said Leemu who was also supported by a missionary family. "Today, when people look at us, they feel that our parents paid all the thousands of dollars for our education. Those people who brought us up were doing it for our people and ourselves."

While Dr. Kiamu and his wife were conversing, they opened the front door that Friday morning. They saw Suah sitting on their porch with bags of rice, cassava, eddoes, and charcoal along with a live red rooster, and a gallon of palm oil from Payeta.

Leemu greeted Suah as Latto and Manu jumped on her lap while she was sitting on a bamboo bench by the wall.

"How long have you been here?" asked Dr. Kiamu.

"A couple of hours, Sir," she replied.

"Why didn't you knock at the door?"

"I really didn't want to do that. Thinking that you were still in bed, and knowing that you would eventually come out when the cook comes for you to open the door for her; I decided to remain, taking some morning breeze, since we had a long walk this morning."

"Oh no, Neh Suah!" Dr. Kiamu replied, "You shouldn't have gone through all of that. You are no longer a stranger to us. I take you to be like my sister. I think you are surprised that I called you, 'Neh Suah,' which means, 'mother Suah.' That was how tradition taught us to call older or all women by putting 'Neh' or 'mother' before their names. Do not be surprised. I am still used to my tradition. I may frequently call you Neh Suah. That should not be misinterpreted that I am making you to appear older."

"No, doctor, it is not a bad way. It is the same way women were taught to call men by putting 'Nah' or 'father' before their given names. Our culture today allows us to call older people anyway, even by a nickname."

As Dr. Kiamu and Suah conversed, he went and stood near the goods she had brought. He then asked her, "Anyway, how much do you want to sell all of this?"

"No, doctor, what are you saying? I can't be that inhumane to sell them to you. I brought these items for my daughter's friend, Manu. "Living a life isn't a one-way street. If we live to receive and never to give back something, then we are not living in the world that needs our individual and collective contributions. We live by showing a little kindness to one another. I don't want to wait any longer in thanking you for the unique care you have given to Latto. Only the Lord will reward you."

"You don't have to say all of that. We are obligated to do that for people.

"Thank you," Dr. Kiamu reciprocated. "But Mommy, you don't have to bring these items for free. You are farming, and you need some money. You can't give these goods free to us..."

"No! I'm beginning to think that you don't want us to continue the friendship on a good foot, doctor," Suah interrupted Dr. Kiamu.

Everybody laughed at her.

"I say again kindness is reciprocal. Only the dead man can't reciprocate kindness. There is no poor man or rich man in giving. I brought these items purposely for you. I didn't bring them for sale. I'm obligated to thank you for the way you have cared for Latto. Her father wished to come with me, but he went on an urgent trip." (In reality, Suah refused to say the truth. Instead, she protected her home without saying that her husband cared less about other things except for his drinking, smoking, and pacing around the place).

After having lunch with Dr. Kiamu and his family, Leemu said, "Suah, I beg that you and Latto shouldn't go today. We want you to stay and spend some time with us as we have done with Latto."

"Since it would be one night it wouldn't be a problem for me. It is just that I have to go back quickly to see after the other children," Suah replied to Leemu.

"You are right," Dr. Kiamu said.

The Kiamus did not want to abruptly discuss issues about Latto when they hadn't engaged her mother in other friendly discussions during the day.

In the afternoon, they had a ride to Lewisville. The Kiamus brought some foodstuff along and gave some nice clothes for Suah and a well designed shirt and a pair of shoes for her husband.

That evening they had a supper with rice, cassava leaf, deer meat and palm oil. During the same night Dr. Kiamu called the attention of Suah and informed her that they have eagerly waited to see her come back once again to their home. He thanked her for bringing up Latto to be a wonderful and beautiful child. He and his wife had observed the child to be a hardworking child. They did not believe that there would be any problem for somebody to give any assistance to her.

Dr. Kiamu continued, "Let me tell you something, Neh Suah. For the few days your daughter has spent with us, we are so happy with her attitude. We don't want this potentially talented little child to be denied the chance to go to school. It is education that separates us from the other class of animals. It is education that carries us to the world unknown. It enlightens our minds and develops our surroundings. If we educate our children like the white man is doing, ignorance, disease and poverty won't be around us tomorrow. Our lifespan would be longer than the one an illiterate man lives.

"As we have been blessed with two children, adopting Latto as our third child would be the nicest idea for our family. You are already aware that Manu doesn't have a sister, and she has been crying for Latto. She would be happy to have Latto as her sister."

"Well, no one can refuse when someone is putting soup on his or her rice. This is the opportunity I have been looking for," said Suah as she stood up and shook hands with Dr. Kiamu and Leemu. "As our people always say, 'no one person can train a child.' When we were growing up, the community members reprimanded or commended us, depending on what we did."

She said, "It was the responsibility of everybody to care for the orphans and the wayward children. There was no difference among children. No parent was condemned for putting another person's child on the right path. The community was a family system with common norms, which squared up with everybody, including the children and the elderly people.

"I'm impressed with the way you have taken care of Latto. I don't have any fear in entrusting you with her. The only thing I beg for is I don't want Latto to be called an adopted child. I want you to take her to be like your biological child. Appreciating her like your own child will make her open up to you and to do well in everything."

"Oh, don't worry about that, Ma'am," Leemu accepted. "We will try our best, even though as human beings, we aren't a hundred percent perfect. As parents, we will make sure that all our children are cared for and disciplined accordingly."

"She is a respectful child," Suah bragged. "I have made her get used to moral living. I'm hoping that she will try to live by those teachings. When I go back I will explain everything to my people."

"By the grace of God, you will live long and you will see Latto as one of the outstanding women in the world," Dr. Kiamu promised.

"I hope so," Suah said.

"Latto, please come closer, let me give you the blessing our ancestors always gave to their younger ones," Suah said.

Latto grinned at her mother, following all the traditional norms.

"When you were born, my late mother, Neh Korto named you Latto as the person who will spread our name to the outside world. Now, it is that time.

"In a similar way, I'm blessing you before I leave you. I'm sure you will behave with these people. When they try to correct you for what you might have done wrong, please do not talk back to them. You have to play the fool sometimes to develop yourself. Working hard and taking directions from good people will make you be a refined person."

Latto smiled as she remained, kneeling before her mother.

She continued, "Please work honestly for all that you will own. Always be reverent to those to whom respect and honor are due. Pay your allegiance to laws and authorities.

"Look in the eyes of people and tell them the truth, not just half of the truth, but the whole truth. Do not say the truth because the truth will make you free and give you life everlasting, but say the truth because God demands it from you, society needs it from you, and it helps you to set up precedence as the rule of the game. As you conform yourself to be faithful by being truthful, you are building up a chain of truth-sayers. The society will continue to have truth-sayers after you have left the stage of truth-saying.

"Don't be arrogant to people who have control over your life or overlook anybody you think you are better off than. Be just with people and walk humbly with the Lord. Protect the name of our village, our family, and yourself. Give the meaning of life to the needy. You will go around this world. Remember our home—Payeta, the land where you were born. Don't forget your roots. The Lord will put you at the head of your ambition, if you follow the tradition of our ancestors, fulfill my dream and learn from my mistakes.

"Anything which you have not encountered nor seen, you should not argue about it, nor say it can't happen to you. Even if you encounter such a thing, know that it is only similar but not exactly as it had happened to others. Each of us lives each day by the mercy and the blessing of God. Before we receive our blessings beyond every other blessing we pray to live right and dutiful. None of us is better than the other."

Latto said, "Don't worry, mother. By God's grace, I will do according to all these commendations that you are giving me. You are putting me on your blessing road. The Lord of the heavens will continue to bless your lass to bring back blessings from this trip."

Suah concluded, "I will continue to pray that our ancestors continue to ask the Lord to pour the dews of the heavens upon your heritage and your womb. The Lord will cause your enemies to support your grounds."

Latto got up and leaned on her mother as they both hugged and wept copiously.

Chapter 9

Several days had passed. Things had been going smoothly according to the expectation of the Kiamu family, helping them to reach their conclusion about their next plan for Latto.

Dr. Kiamu had discovered that investing in any human being, like his family was the same for Latto, it would have a long lasting impact on the recipient and many other persons who are involved. Several experiences led him to also believe that most people who have the means are not encouraged nowadays to help people who seem to be in need. The nonserious attitudes of most young people to pursue their aspirations had discouraged people who are willing to help them, because nobody wants to use his or her little resources behind nonserious people.

As Dr. Kiamu and his wife were aware of the risk by providing for Latto, they decided to provide an opportunity for Latto, which would also benefit her family and the surrounding villagers. They believed that educating more children, especially girls in Leewah, was an enormous undertaking, which would make the region to be one of the best regions in the world.

Building their hopes that Suah and her family would place the care of Latto in their hands worried Dr. Kiamu and his wife through the night. They prayed that the Lord would speak to the hearts of Suah and her people to allow the opportunity to be utilized.

Any reverse action to their plan would be discouraging to his family, especially Manu, who had put all her attention into getting a sister. The Kiamus continued to look at one another with a deeper compassion for Latto and her family.

Dr. Kiamu knew that the absence of any family member like Latto is a dreadful sorrow for the rest of family. "It takes some time before they can overcome the trauma," he said, "We are looking up to God to provide us with this child." He also believed that wise thinkers in the family would embrace the idea that it is a worthy investment to let the child go out and receive the best knowledge in order to improve the living standard of her people.

"I always tell you that the Lord has his timing for everything," Leemu informed her husband. "A colonial proverb says, 'what is for you will surely see your face before your death.' I knew we could get a submissive child one day. I am sure the Lord had already given us one."

"Now, we must fulfill all legal requirements as quickly as possible," Dr. Kiamu informed his wife.

"What legal requirements?" she asked grudgingly.

"You know that raising another person's child without proper documentation isn't the right idea. A family who intends to raise a child must have a legal custody over that child."

"That's true Daddy, but not in the case of our own people. I don't think that is necessary."

"No, honey, you heard Suah when she said that we should take the girl as our own."

"We can't take her words letter by letter. We have our own way of demonstrating our affections for people. I'm concerned that when we adopt her, it will be written in the document that she's an adopted child."

"I don't think she meant that we shouldn't have some legal documents for her. You know that we live in a sophisticated world. Who knows some day, we might be asked somewhere to verify whether all the children are our biological children.

"If we go contrary to the requirement then we must have legal backing, or we could be made of shame."

"That's true," she said. "Let's go ahead and do the right thing as you proposed."

"I can see that you seem to be overwhelmed. I believe adoption is the heart of divinity. It changes any family dynamic. If you love your adopted child, perhaps your biological children or kinsmen may or may not love the child the same way. Your proof is always the legal custody you have obtained," Dr. Kiamu stated.

"That philosophy is contrary to our family's gospel. Our children already love Latto. In fact, they are the ones who are bringing Latto into this home. There won't be any conflicting issue for them."

"I don't mean my children. I mean society, including her parents. They are going to watch us for the way we are taking care of their child.

"Do we care about that?"

"No! Sometimes, the world sees you more than you watch yourself."

"Then why must we worry about them instead of the child?"

"People learn from others' actions. Do you still remember Becky, the lady who was the Godmother for Numeh? Becky and her husband adopted Erica at the age of five from a poverty stricken village. Erica seemed to be a nice little girl. She had been serious with her education. Her adoptive family was very impressed.

"In fact, Erica's family always told Becky that their daughter had no other relatives anywhere. Both families had become one family.

"But a relative who had not been involved in little Erica's life began, giving her money and doing things secretly for her. As a result, Erica finally left Becky and her husband and went back to her village. Today, Erica has six children with a seventh grade education, single mother and having no means of income to support herself or her family."

"Latto is my child. In the first place, I don't think we are getting the child to please other people, including my own people. I'm getting her for my own comfort. Also, I'm a mother, and educated as well. Nobody will dictate to me on how to care for my children," Leemu concluded.

Chapter 10

The Sunday after Suah went home, Dr. Kiamu and his wife went to Payeta to officially adopt Latto.

When some villagers had seen Dr. Kiamu and his team enter the village, they gathered at the town square, jubilating for the arrival of the humanitarian educator.

"I'm so pleased to have Dr. Kiamu along with his wife, visiting us today," Chief Dokpa Jao said after commanding the Town Crier, Senatuah, to assemble every resident to the town square.

The chief recalled that the couple has helped lots of communities in the region during the past seven years of work at the hospital and school of nursing. He also observed that they had personally donated funds and other resources for the construction of schools, clinics, and farm-to-market roads in most villages, including their birth village, which was built on a mountain.

"No day will be remembered like this day," Chief Jao said as he continued to shake Dr. Kiamu's hand with joy. "This man cannot come to any town without having a project in mind for that town. I know he has come with some good news for our village."

The villagers paid keen attention to the chief. They gathered under the palaver hut, which was used as the civil court. The traditional white kola nuts were placed in a calabash and passed around.

All the people in the audience had a bite of the kola nuts as a sign of driving away the evil spirits among them. Unwilling people were rebuked to take bites of the kola nuts or else they were presumed to have evil minds as those who always obstructed the development of their surroundings.

After the ritual was performed Dr. Kiamu humbly said, "When you see a lizard comes from a hole with a bloody head, no one can ask it whether there was a bullfrog or a snake in the hole. We have come to you, which means, we have a problem. But, we are officially the guests of Suah and her family. My wife and I decided to bring this sack of clothes for the village. After we have met with them, we will meet you before we leave."

The crowd shouted with joy, and some paced around them as their own way of thanking the couple.

As the chief's representatives were dividing the clothes, Suah's kinsmen had gathered at their house. Dr. Kiamu said, "My wife and I have come to officially declare our intention that we need Latto as our child."

During a series of discussions behind closed doors, Torkolon, an influential uncle of Latto and the younger brother of Yallon, stood up and said, "Look all around us. Have you seen any educated female lawyers or judges in our society? Where have you seen people sending women to school black man sending his girl-child to white man's school?

"If Dr. Kiamu wants to help, it would be better for him to help some of our boys. He has some ulterior reasons for wanting to adopt a girl. You will not understand his intention. Those fools always want girls. When the girls have grown up, then they become their secret concubines, their sex slaves or later divorce their wives to marry them."

All the kinsmen roared at Torkolon with murmurings heard everywhere.

Then, Myron advanced himself in the middle of the audience and quieted them to put some sense in Torkolon's head. "Stop your hate talks. Stop your foolish and narrow-mindedness. Have you not seen educated white and black women taking care of you in many ways? Who is Mrs. Kiamu? Is she not a woman, a black woman? When you, your children or your relatives are sick and go to the hospital, how do you consider those who do the treatments? See the villagers around us doing what Dr. Kiamu wants to do for us. It is absurd that you can even think like a stupid novice," he said. "You are evil in everything and in all your doings. You have got all those beautiful children and you do not want to send any of them to school. Why can't someone do what you have failed to do? Do you want the same thing to happen to your brother's children? The child we are talking about is my sister's daughter. By tradition, I have a greater voice in the affairs of my sister's children than even the man who born them by my sister. What kind of human being are you? Have you not learned that it is good to talk nice about others? How can you talk like those who haven't gone anywhere? I wonder if you ever graduated from our manhood training. If you did, you couldn't have talked like a novice. I would strongly recommend that our elders engage themselves to do some work with you."

The whole group of kinsmen praised Myron as they condemned Torkolon. Nuwoe also begged for his brother. He persuaded Torkolon to find his senses and to apologize, too. Later, Torkolon remained quiet with his disgrace.

The kinsmen came back and agreed that Latto should be adopted. The chance was given to Myron, who was crippled in both limbs, a junior zoë of the village, to perform the traditional family ritual.

He called Latto to come closer.

As Latto made the attempt to squat, Neh Tamay, a maternal cousin of Suah, ordered her to prostrate before Myron. She laid herself on the floor for her blessing.

While performing the family ritual, Myron skillfully chanted the names of their ancestors to remit blessings from the Lord to Latto. Since he was the oldest living kinsman, he was endowed with the responsibility to do so. He slaughtered a white rooster and poured the blood on the jewelry of their ancestors in a calabash that had been passed from one generation to the other. He rubbed some of the blood on Latto's head. He also poured his saliva on her head and in her both palms. He told her to rub it on her forehead.

"When you step on any stone, let it be under your feet like a rotten banana. Wherever you go in this world, let fortune follow you like the pollinator flies or as easy as the twinkling of an eye," he said as he carried on another long chanting. At the end, all the kinsmen responded.

"This is the highest blessing for you. It's only bestowed upon obedient children," Myron said. "I pray that any obstacle that comes along your way shall be blown away by the power of the Lord. I bless you with the voices of our long-gone ancestors."

Feeling happy with the blessing, Latto uttered, "Amen." It was her own way of responding to her uncle's customary ritual. Others who were present applauded for the smooth process of the sacred ceremony.

After the family meeting, Suah and her family along with Dr. Kiamu and his wife joined the other town people to perform the official rite of the adoption.

Suah and her family informed the town chief and his councilmen of their intention to allow Latto to be adopted.

Town chief Jao informed his councilmen and the elders, including other citizens to officially approve the adoption. He gave Dr. Kiamu and his wife all the legal documents to legalize the start of a lasting union.

"No agreement of this nature has been done in this village without a sacred ceremony," said Chief Dokpa Jiao. "Kill me the white sheep along with some roosters for the official traditional feast. Everybody present here today must take part in this traditional sacrifice for Latto's protection. Any refusal means that the person is keeping some evil thoughts in his or her mind about Latto."

He went and stood in the middle of the audience and said, "Doctor, let me say this to you and your wife. When you do not tell the truth to your potential lover in the first days of acquaintance, she will not trust you at any time. We give you this child with our whole hearts. We aspire that our children's lives should be better than ours. Children should be in the position to one day bury their parents honorably instead of their parents living better lives than the children. We know that the time has come for us to receive help through you, sir. Please put the best of life in our child."

He stared at Dr. Kiamu and his wife, and said, "Even though we hadn't sent any of our children, especially girls to school, we have always believed that one day, we will send them to school. We thought that the white man's education was strange and immorally unacceptable for women. But while attending a development meeting a few weeks ago, I learned that education in all of its forms was highly important for every man and woman. 'When you educate men, you have educated individuals, but when you educate women you have educated the entire nation.' The moderator of the meeting said that lazy and uneducated parents do not make the future bright for their children. 'Equally so, it is not the truth to life that a parent should be educated more than his or her child,' he said. 'Children have at least two groups of people to look up to for any assistance: the parents and themselves.' Our children should not be losers when we are there to make things better for their future."

The chief continued, "Even though I don't have any young child, my approach towards the white man's education has changed. I encourage the young people who are bearing children in this village to send all of them to school without any discrimination. As Dr. Kiamu is starting it for us, we must reciprocate it by producing palm oil or farming to send our children to school. Life today will not remain like this forever.

"That was how people in other parts of the world were able to develop their communities. They never performed any special magic. Seriousness and helping one another developed their nations. We are their slaves today because we failed to help ourselves. We are no longer taken away by the means of the trans-Atlantic or Trans-Saharan slave Trade. Each day we are forcing ourselves to be slaves. We have neglected to develop our land. We have failed to help one another, our children and others. We can only stop being slaves, if we will realize and follow what Dr. Kiamu is doing."

He gazed at Dr. Kiamu and finally said, "Doctor, our blessings and the blessings of the Lord be with you, your family as well as your newly adopted daughter!"

Then, Dr. Kiamu answered, "Chief Jao, many thanks to you and your councilmen. Your words are well taken into our hearts. Let us wish for the better days. Man cannot roar for his aspiration like a jungle lion or a machine gun. By the grace of God, we will try our best for Latto."

Chapter 11

A few days after returning from Payeta for the adoption, the Kiamus registered Latto at Garrison, a government school situated in Jamesburg a few miles from the hospital. They bought her all the necessary school supplies to be prepared just like an elite child.

"I'm so happy about my opportunity for my education," Latto thought. "I wish I had started my education long ago. Anyway, it is not too late for me to learn. This family has a good plan for me."

As a polite person, Manu had taught her newly adopted sister how to read and write the English alphabet. Latto had mastered all that her sister had taught her.

When Latto went to school the first day, she saw no child from Payeta in the school. She felt somehow discouraged about that. Such a discouragement taught her to set a good example for her village.

During the first day of school Mrs. Collins, who was the kindergarten teacher with a very good colonial accent wrote the English alphabet on the blackboard and called on Latto to read.

Latto read each letter perfectly, better than the majority of the pupils who had been in school for a long time. "Please come with me to my office," said Mrs. Collins.

As Mrs. Collins made Latto to sit adjacent to her in her office, she said, "You seem to be serious about your education, little girl. Please continue with your studies. Education is an individual business. Your parents may pay all your fees, but they will not learn for you. Putting your mind into your learning is the best secret for education.

"Who are your parents?" she asked.

"Dr. Frula Kiamu and his wife, Leemu Kiamu, both work with the hospital across the road."

"You will be one of the future leaders of the world," she observed.

When Latto reached home, her mother saw the joy in her face. She knew that the first day of Latto's education was a joyous one.

Latto greeted and informed her mother that Mrs. Luoda Collins was her teacher. "She made me her friend," she said. "She told me how she got her education. She showed me her family's pictures, too."

"Great!" Leemu said as she browsed through her daughter's notebook. "Mrs. Collins always likes smart pupils. Maybe she sees you like that.

"Wait a minute! Is this your writing? Have you been to school before?"

"No, Ma'am."

"Wow, you mean during the two weeks you have spent here, you have learned all of that?" Leemu seemed overwhelmed by the young village girl's ambition for learning.

"Yes, Mommy," she replied with a smile as she glanced at Leemu. "Manu has been a great help for me. She had taught me all these things every day."

"That's amazing. You are a genius. You and your sister will do something...Go and change your uniform," commanded Leemu as she noted Latto's uniform still looked neat like she hadn't worn it.

Latto quickly hopped with joy as she disappeared from her mother and joined Manu and Numeh who were already playing in the backyard.

"Thank you so much sister for teaching me those lessons. They were a great help for me today," she said, showing the class exercises to Manu.

"I guess you weren't shy about doing any class work?" Manu asked, "How do you feel?"

"You know sister; before a man's hair is burned, the beard burns first, it is the beard he hangs over the fire. It isn't an easy thing to be introduced to a new way of life for the first day. My legs were waggling with fears when I was called to the chalkboard to read the exercise.

"Lots of fears grabbed at my mind, but I fought against the fear of making a mistake, the fear of failure, the fear against my self-esteem, and the fear of losing my confidence or trust with the teacher. However, I read every exercise perfectly and with confidence," Latto said.

"That happens to everybody," Manu concurred. "It happened to me several times when I started school. I was among bigger children whom I thought knew more.

"I stood boldly to answer any question. By doing that, the fear went away from me. Several times my teacher pointed at me to answer the most difficult questions. I had no fear to answer since I studied my lessons at home before going to bed. I didn't spend endless time on flipping channels and watching television or having botched conversations."

"Now, I see why Daddy is so proud about you," Latto said.

"Which parent doesn't like to see his or her child doing things better?" asked Numeh.

"Only careless parents would do that. Loving parents, whether they are poor or not, will always make some sort of initiation for their children," Latto replied.

"I tell you, my dad always gives me prizes when I do well in my lessons. That support has always given me more strength to go in for the difficult tasks in my learning," Manu said. "My dad always says that a child who does something good, earns himself or herself a good reward; equally so with the child who does something wrong must be reprimanded."

"My mother always does the same thing in another way for me. Whenever I help her, she always does something good in return for me. She will say that a well-behaved child brings blessings to the parents," Latto added."

Before the end of the next semester, Latto's teacher discovered certain dishonesty in her work. She called her before the class. "I'm not satisfied with your work."

Latto looked at the teacher and placed her finger in her mouth, appearing confused about what her teacher was talking about.

She was afraid to express herself due to her limited English vocabulary.

The teacher suggested, "To resolve the problem, you will take the test over in front of me now."

When the teacher asked Latto the first question, she recited the entire notes instead of answering just the one question.

Then the teacher said, "I see why they gave you the promotion. How is it possible for you to memorize a whole note? You are okay, go and take your seat."

At the end of the first semester Latto received a double promotion along with some other students.

She went home with pride and dignity again.

This time, when her father received the report, he said to Latto, "I'm happy about your report card. We will spend more time helping you to improve your English and your learning skills. I will design a program for you."

For each letter of the alphabet, he wrote ten words containing one syllabus. Manu made sure that Latto master the assignment within two months before her school opened.

Chapter 12

There had been no time as important to Latto as the time Dr. Kiamu involved himself in her education. They had built a cordial relationship as father and daughter.

During the break, Dr. Kiamu prepared over two thousand words for Latto to learn as part of his effort. In no time, Latto had memorized them.

When the second semester commenced, like most children from little towns, unable to express themselves in the English Language fluently, Latto would sit quietly in a back corner of the class to pay attention to her lessons, while most of the pupils who had failed in the same class were running all over the place, knocking on the tables, the chairs, and throwing dusters at one another.

Once again, Mrs. Roberts, the second grade teacher wasn't around. Her class was disturbing the entire school.

It caught the attention of Rosa, the principal. She wrote a sentence on the chalkboard:

"I am the Principal of this school, I need no noise!"

From the teacher's desk near the chalkboard to the last desk at the rear, Rosa lined up all the students in the classroom. She began to call them one by one.

Almost no one in the entire class read the sentence correctly.

"I remember Manu told me what to do whenever there is a fear," said Latto. "She told me to think beyond the given task. She also told me that whenever I'm asked to read or to do any job, I must say to myself, 'I can do it,' and take a deep breath to overcome the fear. That's the way I can regain courage."

After Latto had read the sentence perfectly, Rosa got excited. "You are one of the youngest persons among the pupils. You seem to be more serious than some of these grown up men and women."

Latto appeared timid, but happy when Rosa held her hand and led her into the third grade class. She introduced her to Mrs. Morrison, who had made the third grade class the toughest class in Garrison. Most students hardly passed her class. The aggressive students had been punished or expelled from the school because of their continual failure and reaction against Mrs. Morrison.

Before this time, there had been no one promoted in the history of Garrison School by a principal of a pupil like Rosa did to Latto. She went even further by giving her some money. She said to her, "Go and buy a new uniform, since you won't use this one for your new class."

As Latto was rejoicing in her mind, several female students gathered around her during the recess period. Some admired her, while the radical ones scolded her about her achievement. "What is your secret, what makes you excel in all your classes?" They asked, "Is there some sort of demonic power, making you to do all these things? We see you do not even speak a Standard English. Where in this world would you village girl get the brain to pass all lessons, if you were not dealing with some kind of supernatural beings?"

Latto sat quietly and listened to all the utterances and condemnations from her colleagues. She felt sad about her inability to express herself fluently in English. She tried, however, her best however and said to her challengers, "There is no special medicine for education."

"Then, how do you always manage to pass all your tests? I'm guessing a certain supernatural being somewhere gave you a special brain better than ours," one of them said.

"I'm still young, having no boyfriend to spend endless time with or children to distract my attention from my lesson. I have a clean bill of health. I live with my parents, and they provide all my needs.

"Why can't I study my lessons and make better grades in school? Let me tell all of you, only dumb-headed people can neglect to burn their candles or lanterns at night to put some knowledge in their skulls. I don't think you people are some of them. God gave you skulls and you have refused to fill them with knowledge. I do not want to be like you. That is why I fill my skull with the best knowledge. Do not forget, one day some of you will be our servants, if you continue this trend of bullying people and not being serious about your lessons."

The place became quiet as Latto walked out of their presence and entered the class to finish the balance of the school day.

After school, Latto immediately went home and shared the joy with her sister and brother as well as her parents.

Dr. Kiamu was so astonished about the progress of his daughter and said, "Latto, I believe you need a present for all your great accomplishments, especially your double promotion and your birthday."

"Yes, thank you, Dad!"

"I told you that about Dad," Manu said.

"What do you need?" he asked. He came and stood by the children, who were busy with their mother, picking up her few strands of gray hair.

Manu went closer to their father and said, "Daddy, Latto is shy to tell you what we have discussed."

"And what have you discussed? Tell me! I want to know. Don't feel frightened."

"Latto wants to see the National Waterfall. I showed her the pictures we took last year. She hasn't seen such a thing like a waterfall before," Manu said.

Leemu, who seemed to be interested in the discussion, said, "Daddy, it's a nice idea. If you agree to their suggestion, they could see the waterfall and the mysterious areas around there. They would take a van ride to see the historic monkey village and the rocky mountain town."

Dr. Kiamu joked, "Okay, you and your children have bought me. Ladies are peculiar people. When they talk, no man talks or else, he would spend good time somewhere else."

"So, you say! That is why we are your mothers." His wife said, joyfully.

Then, Dr. Kiamu confirmed the date, "Latto, next Saturday will be your outing at the fall."

The children rushed to their father and hugged him with joy.

“That’s the result of being serious about doing better things in life. Latto deserves it,” said Dr. Kiamu. “It’s our responsibility to encourage each of you to do more. Your mother and I will not relent until we see you graduate from college, so you will continue with your education.”

Chapter 13

After weeks of hectic preparation, the long-expected day for Latto's program had finally arrived. Latto's parents had bought her another nice forest green colored dress with a pair of brown sandals. She wore them to her program on that day with joy and enthusiasm.

Present at the occasion were her principal and teachers, along with the six students who received the double promotions with her. Some of her parents' colleagues from the hospital were also present.

After being informed about her daughter's progress, Suah came to the program along with Chief Jao and some villagers from Payeta. This time, her husband, Yallon, and his two brothers, Torkolon and Nuwoe, and their head wives, Nowah and Yamah were present. They were singing and dancing, throwing grains of rice all over the place.

For Latto's occasion, some well-known educated personalities delivered speeches intended to teach people the importance of better child-care and societal development. One of the speakers among them was a middle-aged lady with the assumed name Dr. Lucia Selma, who had obtained double-doctorate degrees, and was teaching at the nearby private university.

Dr. Selma began her speech with an aphorism, she thought her audience knew the meaning very well. She said, "In life, there are always many rocky roads with many pot holes, curves, and bumps. In other words, everyone has at least one problem that stands as an obstacle in his or her in life. That problem or obstacle could be poverty or illiteracy. The way that person strives to overcome it, turning it into blessings, makes him or her as an outstanding figure in life. Most of the time, only lazy people sit redundantly, procrastinating until their problems overwhelm them. The strong and wise ones, though poor or illiterate, always persevere and strive for the solutions to their problems."

She told the gathering, including Latto that she had a rocky road, too. She said that when she was an innocent teenager, she was overwhelmed with an infatuated love. She had her first child by another teenager from a poor family. She told them that she could not receive enough support from the child's father. She was unable to cater to the child. She considered it as the greatest disgrace she ever brought to her family. "My father made a deal with me, and he said, 'Honey, I know how embarrassed you are. Inasmuch as we are not condoning this act, you deserve a second chance if you will work out an agreement with me.'"

She said, her father continued, "Your mother and I will take care of your child. But only this child will we care for. If you get pregnant again out of wedlock, we will give you this child so that you can care for all your children by yourself. Please consider our offer as the last resort towards your growth and maturity."

"I grieved over the situation but agreed to every bit of what my father had said.

"I chose to start the first grade class at the age of eighteen." She stopped and gazed at the audience to appeal to their emotions and understandings of the idea she was trying to pass onto them.

"Through my seriousness, my father and a local pastor became my closest friends. They constantly nurtured and supported me," she said.

"They were not only in my life, but also through their guidance I was awarded a scholarship and attended one of the outstanding Christian boarding mission high schools in Leewah.

"After I graduated from high school, I traveled overseas to continue my education. However, I didn't have enough money to underwrite the cost of my entire education. I did a personal care with an aging woman. Before her death, the old lady wrote a check for an undisclosed amount of money."

She related, "In the reference section, she wrote, 'Selma, this is for your education.'

"A few months after her death, I unexpectedly received the Bible that contained the money from her, which underwrote all the expenses for my education."

She continued, "Let me let you know that the best time for you to learn is when you are still young—not yet married, no children crying on you here and there, no responsibility. It's good to learn at your age level. I believe that learning starts from the early days of life and progresses into an old age. Learning at the mature stage of life is not advisable. It brings a lot of hurdles for the older person. Learning time can pass for the right purpose and opportunity. I do not mean when a person is old, he should not go to school. When the child is educated at the early age, he or she would have ample time and years to help develop the society.

"The prosperity of any nation is determined by the knowledge of the young people and the wisdom of its senior citizens. I wish leaders of Leewah would prioritize education, instead of thinking about engaging in buying weapons first. Education brings development and eradicates fraud and corruption in the land. "

Dr. Selma asked, "How can the nation prosper when vast majorities of the people who dwell within the nation are uneducated? The active workforce of any nation is between twenty to fifty years, beyond that are people acting as senior consultants.

"I want to leave you, especially Latto whom we are celebrating this day in your honor, with one philosophy. Have the ambition to go for anything, especially for the best in this world. Don't let people dissuade you. In life it is only the persistent strivers whom survive the tides of earthly circumstances. If you can't aim for the head, you will always get the tail.

"I consider education as a wagon. It carries both men and women as equals in progress on the same road, wherever they want to go."

The president of the nation's public university, Dr. Talon Fromo, was the next speaker. He encouraged Latto and others in the audience. He said that God should be the first person to consider in whatever a man does.

Dr. Fromo believed that consulting God for his guidance makes most people successful. He advised that no man should play with his job, because through it he lives. He said, "It's a job that fetches you money for survival. In other words, do any jobs for clean money."

As Latto listened, Dr. Fromo informed them that his blessing came through writing. "I wrote hundreds of letters, explaining my situation as a poor man's son to solicit aid for my education," he said. "Out of that number, one family volunteered to sponsor my education. The second letter I received, it contained a reasonable amount of money. I took a greater portion of it as a sacrifice and then gave some to anybody I found in need along the byways.

"Through their help, I later went abroad, where I obtained a PhD got married, and now have three beautiful children."

Dr. Fromo believed that blessings come in the form of an opportunity, which may surface once in lifetime. When it isn't utilized at the time it appears, it might never come back to that person the same way. He said that it is not advisable for anybody to delay the chance that is at hand. He challenged that if a person ask some of the displaced people in the society, they would say that it was due to some kind of mistake that led them to the place where they are.

"There's no second chance to opportunities, think big and rush in towards whatever you want in life, and you will surely get it in the end. Remember, it is very easy to do the wrong thing rather than doing good things. No decision should be regrettable. Thinking twice before making decisions in life is very much important. Your parents would be the proudest people when they see you are still doing the right thing up to the final hours of their stay on this earth," he concluded.

Rev. Carlue Burwell, the chaplain of the hospital, who appeared as the last speaker, told Latto and others attending her program that the most vulnerable people in this world are children who are not in school. "Most of them are found in the streets, striving for their survival. Most parents neglect to support their children. Building learning facilities in every village and to make it mandatory that all our children are in school should be the priority obligations to government."

He went on to say, "If such an effort is undertaken, very soon every citizen would have the opportunity to read and write. I don't see any reason a nation would prosper if education was downplayed. At least, if everyone knows how to read and write, the meaning of national developmental initiatives would be understood and undertaken. I appeal to our leaders to prioritize education in order to prepare our future leaders. Or else, I am afraid, most of the uneducated citizens of this nation would be our problems, quick to be bought by some educated ones or criminal-minded people to engage into some sort of civil unrest to bring us down."

At the end of the program, knocking on her left breast, believing that it was the first thing that nursed her child a few minutes after her birth, Suah once again whispered to Leemu who sat near her, "I'm grateful for the way things are going with Latto."

Then, Leemu responded, "Let her continue to aim at the sky, one day she will get one of the stars, and we all are going to benefit from it."

Chapter 14

Christmas has always been the biggest holiday that brings people together from all walks of life to celebrate it with their loved ones and family members at home or abroad. It is also the time for old friends to reunite or reconcile their differences, while others find it as a time to get new friends. Whatever the intention, it is a joyous day, but not the day any man should be making commotions in his family or in the neighborhood.

Gathering to celebrate another Christmas were the workers of the Christian hospital, including the residents of Jamesburg and Lewisville as well as the residents of Latto's birth-village of Payeta.

Everything was set up. By the order of Chief Kwegeh, the District Commissioner reinforced by his various town chiefs, all the towns and the villages as well as bridges and roads had been timely reconditioned.

As the people celebrated, they exchanged gifts with one another. Precious livestock that hadn't been eaten or sold during the course of the year was slaughtered to prepare various kinds of delicious meals. Their palatable smells breezed in the atmosphere, making the hungry person to salivate like a strayed dog. Their joyous moods signified that the year had been a productive one.

Appreciating the services of the workers during the course of the year, the hospital had divided meats along with financial bonuses among them.

Dr. Kiamu, who had always rendered kindness to people, especially during the holidays like the Christmas season, making him as one of the outstanding figures of the area, had again invited his colleagues, Dr. Fromo and Dr. Selma along with their families from the nearby Christian college to celebrate the holiday with his family.

But, there was an awful change during the event. The horn, the salsa, and the drum players had stopped performing in the nearby towns. The people, playing on the hospital compound had noticed the change and had gotten concerned.

As Latto noticed the change, too, she ran from the back porch, where she had gone to deposit a trash bag. "Something is happening," she cried out. "People are running everywhere."

Instead of going back to the kitchen where her mother and the cook, Yonkor and her friend, Yarnga was cooking, Latto rushed to Dr. Kiamu who was sitting among his friends, entertaining themselves under the shelter built for the celebration.

She whispered, "Daddy, the rumor that has been circulating here is true. I heard the people say that a certain armed gang has entered the northeastern part of the nation last night. They have killed many people there. They are on their way to this place. If you go to the front side of this house, you will see people still running all over the place or discussing what the news is."

"Latto! Go in to play with your brother and sister for now. Children don't talk like that," Dr. Kiamu quickly advised his daughter, pretending that he didn't know the reality.

He didn't want his guests to be bothered by those silly rumors that had been circulating in the neighborhood. He believed that whenever an effort was made to confirm the rumor, it was always discovered as another scam of Doudiah, the tyrannical leader of Leewah.

Latto went back into the kitchen and stood by her mother and whispered again, "Something bad is happening around here. Every man is on the run, Mommy."

"Like what?" her mother asked as she went toward the window in the living room. She pushed aside the screen and glanced through it. Surprised by the movement of the people outside, she closed back the screen and sped quickly back into the kitchen to inform the other women.

Yarnga, who was one of the cooks for the hospital, stopped gathering the ingredients for the fried rice she was preparing and said, "All the monkeys and the baboons are going to breathe their last breaths together. We had once sung the song, 'native woman born soldier' or 'let the monkey come down.' As we have been considering the soldier as a monkey, now is the time for that monkey to come down, just like the way the pioneers, headed by Rev. Billy Ray, we considered as baboons came down many years ago."

Yonkor responded to Yarnga remorsefully. "If you consider the indigenous sons and daughters in power as monkeys, and the pioneers whom Chief Doudiah overthrew as baboons, and then who are we?"

"We are the common grasshoppers, you know that," said Yonkor

"You should know that if the monkeys and the baboons fight, the grasshoppers can't survive, because their livelihood depends on them."

"Look, my ladies! Is this what we want to argue about? Do you think war is a nice thing to pray for?" asked Leemu as she left the women and rushed under the shelter and whispered to her husband, "Leewah is no longer a safe place, honey. The war is finally here.

"Really?" he asked. "Are you kidding me?"

"Kidding? There is no joke in a snake's mouth. I don't joke with harmful things. We must be on the alert now."

Dr. Kiamu quickly informed his friends that the enemies of progress were already around them. "I have just been informed that there have been shootings in the northeast during the past night," he said.

"Dr. Kiamu, don't believe it! This same rumor had been circulating for over a year now. Don't mind all these scams of Chief Doudiah, the junta leader and his nepotistic followers in power. When they want to eliminate any of their enemies, they usually do this kind of thing as a cover-up," said Dr. Fromo, who was sitting by a gourd of palm wine. As he took off his eyeglasses to wipe the foam of the palm wine from his long beard and mustache, he asked, "Was it not the same scam that led Chief Doudiah to send a reconnaissance team to the northeast to find out about some kind of strange activity in that area some months ago?

"What was the outcome? What else did we hear? Was it not the usual sugarcoated talks? The northeastern provincial leader had repeatedly informed the reconnaissance team that such a rumor wasn't only intended to tarnish the good reputations of the citizens of the northeastern region, but to jeopardize the progressive development of the area. He emphasized that such a rumor was blatantly unfounded and untrue that they were allowing someone to use their borders for an uprising among the people of Leewah.

"And, while the reconnaissance team was flying back to the capital to report their findings to the boss, Chief Doudiah, it had a crash along the Atlantic coast. The crash produced the fatal deaths of all the occupants of that military plane, piloted by one of my church members and friends, Elder Gamoyu."

"Who doesn't remember that news?" Dr. Kiamu asked. "Everyone knows how poor Massah lost her newly-wedded husband, Elder Gamoyu, in that crash. Today, even though Massah lives in the most popular nation on earth, she is still in pain over the death of that gallant Christian soldier. She's still unmarried, battling to support herself and her two children, wondering why the Lord allowed such a thing to happen to her family.

"I can't understand most of our leaders of this land. Most of them behave like a bunch of rogues or murderers who do not care for the people they came to liberate. If more people die, it does not bother them. Maybe, they want the Lord to come again to put some humanitarian love in their skulls before they can do the right things."

Dr. Selma, who had been keenly listening, added, "Of course, Dr. Kiamu, but since the Lord was here the first time, have they ever listened to him? What will the Lord do different from what he did earlier for humanity? Most people are still continuing to do evil things even worse than the ancient days? Unless they hear that all the gods are dead, perhaps it would be the time for them to think about the heavenly God and to stop the wickedness."

"One thing I know, for certain, there are always elements of truth in every rumor," she said.

"Some of our brothers and sisters abroad had been preparing. They had been buying weapons and getting support from everywhere for this war for years," Dr. Selma informed her colleagues as she placed her glass of palm wine on the little wooden stool at the end of the couch.

Carrying herself closer to Dr. Fromo, she added, "Our people always say, 'it is impossible for anyone to keep news away from others.' I'd heard this news many months ago. What your family is saying is true, Dr. Kiamu. You may not believe it. Each time I tell my colleagues at the college that this nation will soon become a no man's land, they always dispute me. You know over the years, Chief Doudiah has killed lots of his deputies, who were always planning to topple his government. Each time, they miss him; he becomes more aggressive and resentful. You can see half of the national budget is now going for military hardware and war propaganda."

Dr. Fromo went on to add, "Everyone knows that it's the fact. I just hope whatever they want to do it should not be accomplished during our time. We have suffered a lot in this nation. Every generation during the past decades had experienced all kinds of injustices performed by unpatriotic leaders from both pioneers and indigenous people.

"For instance, I lost my cousin and my beloved brother during the so-called Food Riots provoked earlier by some of our returned brothers and sisters from abroad, which took away hundreds of lives. As you are aware, it was just such a struggle that eventually bought Chief Doudiah to power a year later."

Dr. Kiamu supported, "There are still dark clouds about how Chief Doudiah and his group of inexperienced lads, guarding various elite pioneers' homes, came to power overnight. How did they manage to quiet the powerful Rev. Billy Ray and his trained body-guards? Did they know the various places in the state building? How many of their superior officers had ever been around that house before such enlisted men could have penetrated their way to success if a godfather did not have a wishful hand into the planning and the implementation of their struggle?

Dr. Fromo responded, "Who knows? Who is there to doubt or to believe those unsophisticated boys? Who could have given them the means to take over a government that was well supported by international leaders and organizations?"

Dr. Kiamu added, "Since most people, especially the indigenous educated sons and daughters in Leewah expected such an uprising against the elite-classed government of Rev. Billy Ray, no matter who helped them, they were satisfied. Since their minds were made up, they wished everything, except Rev. Billy Ray. Even though he might have been the person who helped most of them to acquire a western education, their eyes were blind to the facts. One of them, the former first chief law enforcer of Doudiah Government testified before a certain peace council, alleging that it was not Chief Doudiah and his men who killed Rev. Billy Ray. He was later rebuked by another former minister of the same government before the same peace council. It is one of the hidden mysteries, only God knows the cause of everything, and he will reveal the truth to the people of Leewah and the world one day."

Dr. Selma said, "Dr. Kiamu, this is not a secret except that it has not been publicly recognized or said by a person in the international community. Who was the Unknown Man, whose portrait was mounted around here some years ago? You must think about that. Just like the way those who supported the pioneers brought them down because of their presumed boorish behaviors, it will be the same way Chief Doudiah and his loyalists will be brought down by their supporters and their intransigent tribesmen."

Dr. Fromo added, "The days of Chief Doudiah are numbered. Killing innocent students in an August raid at a public university campus was ridiculous. Putting student leaders in jail without cause was the worst thing any leader could have done. Attempting to raid neighboring states was not a good idea to maintain the good relations with the neighbors that his predecessors had established. Attempting to wipe out the entire tribe from the northeast in a November raid and killing permanent people was inhumane. Killing some of his main loyalists without the due process of law in a court was absurd. Insulting our step-mother nation was also uncalled for. Secretly hauling away a huge sum of money from nation's treasury and giving it to an individual abroad but in his name was one of the notorious rifts in the nation. Seizing people's wives and daughters without remorse about whose feeling he was hurting was cruel. Allowing no individual or news organization to document him, should teach any wise person that such activities by Chief Doudiah were the official start of the hate-game against him. Most leaders within the sub-region are no longer his comrades, but his contending enemies, risking their lives and resources to see him come down."

He continued, "Even during a regional meeting, a powerful leader from the north challenged Chief Doudiah. He walked to the podium, he looked at Chief Doudiah and said, 'If some of your people have been shooting you with the biggest machine guns in your nation and you have continued to survive them, then you must just allow me to try with my single-barrel gun. Let me see whether you will survive it. Being a leader does not mean to instill fear by lying to the people you are leading or to corrupt the political system for self-gains. This is one of the reasons I advocate that this whole region should be led by one centralized government with all the basic civil services being decentralized.' Another regional leader, on two separate occasions, told Chief Doudiah, 'you can mount all your biggest weapons at my various borders, I will not bother you. When you get tired, the same way you brought them there, it will be the same way you will carry them back to the places where you took them from. You, little lad need to grow up so you know how to respect your elders and others.'"

Dr. Selma answered, "Going back to the history of this land, there has always been a series of minor tribal, pioneer, and indigenous disputes as well as oppression and the random abuse of human rights and dignity by the leading elites. Even, in the early nineteen century, Leewah was considered among equals as one of the most dehumanizing states of the time. There were continual rigged elections' results, slavery, culture of corruption, and educational disparity. Impunity has always encouraged the constant human rights violations and the nation's obligation to instill justice and freedom among the general populace. Every man became a victim of one thing or the other."

Dr. Fromo said, "I am not praying for an evil. But I can see into the future, Chief Doudiah will surely pay for all these crimes he has committed with his precious blood, too. What sin is ever left unpunished?"

Dr. Kiamu stood at the left side of the shelter and watched the residents in the compound, standing in groups, discussing the odd news. But, some seemed to be jubilant; especially those who had lost some of their family members. They believed that the gangsters who were disrupting the northeast were coming to destroy Chief Doudiah and his loyal followers.

"Let's not pray for it. This nation has experienced the first deadly coup ten years ago that destroyed many lives and properties. It took several months for things to come back to normal," Dr. Selma advised.

Dr. Kiamu retorted that since those ten years, nothing had been normal. "Prominent people continued to die secretly and publicly," he said. "Should an inhumane behavior cause wars upon wars? How hard is it to be wicked as compared to be a good person? It is difficult to learn how to be good, but it doesn't take any time to be a wicked person. There is no store to buy a wicked behavior. But there are many institutions that prepare people to be good people. It was easy for Chief Doudiah to order 'let them move or be removed,' killing and wounding many innocent students. But it was hard for him to say, 'let us support and give free education to all the young people of this nation.'

"We must be prepared to take good care of our families. As I see it, this struggle won't be a short time event. Many people have been affected by the deeds and actions of most of our leaders for a long time. Many people will find this unrest as a way to breed their anger and to enrich themselves."

He said, "Most of our leaders should be responsible for all these issues. They have made enemies with our bordering nations, nations in the sub-regions and even the international nations. I don't think when things get worse anybody or any nation will come to our cry until Chief Doudiah is toppled."

Dr. Fromo revealed, "My friends, this is a serious problem. This is the time our nation, through the auspices of our various organizations should be conducting community revivals, educating the citizenry, especially the young people on how to respond to this dire unrest in a peaceful manner. The religious organizations should meet with the state leaders to assure them of their cooperation about maintaining peace within the nation. They should liaise with international nations to protect the interest of the citizenry and those who are residing within our gates."

"Dr. Fromo, I dearly respect your opinion. Let me say that stubborn people are narrow-minded people. Do we know how many times religious leaders and advocacy groups have pleaded with these blood-thirsty leaders to do the right thing and their voices have not been heard? Have you not heard the rumor that a senior prophetess of a renowned denomination in this nation was secretly killed by Chief Doudiah because she rebuked him for the many killings in the nation?" Dr. Selma said. "Most leaders are also like that. They find it as a defeat and cowardly to succumb to the threats of any adversary."

"Well, we will continue to pray for the best. Only the Lord knows why we must face this kind of situation during the prime of our time. Some of us will survive it and we will have stories to tell our unborn children tomorrow," said Dr. Kiamu as he regretfully went to the kitchen to check on his family and the other ladies who had almost finished, preparing the food for the mid-day Christmas party.

Chapter 15

Having no plan to end the conflict, General Mullah had recruited more men and women into his armed gang. Some of the women were used as his sex objects or servants. Latto and her family watched the continual destruction and the senseless killing. They had seen no reservation in these criminals' minds about the lasting loss of the material and the human resources of the land, which once stood as the beacon of hope for those who were oppressed from other lands.

Latto and her people believed that losing the entire nation meant nothing to General Mullah and his killing squad, once their aims and objectives were accomplished. They never bothered to protect the people, even their own people or their aging parents.

Like every other person in the land and elsewhere, Latto never knew that kind of cruelty could last all these years. "Fourteen is not a small number," she said. "For any nation to be denied all rights, while other nations are developing overnight should be considered as one of the dehumanizing mechanisms invented by people who don't love their motherlands or value other human beings. Some of the people who resented the deeds of General Mullah and his allies always asked, 'where will the funds come from to develop our nation to its original level before reaching the level that other countries have already reached?'"

Latto lamented about her life and the future of her nation as well as that of her biological parents and her siblings whom she had not met or heard from them since the start of the unrest.

She alleged that General Mullah had many kings and queens as well as individuals and organizations, wishing him to remove Chief Doudiah and to destabilize the sub-region in exchange for the natural resources. "Once General Mullah gives them a piece of diamond in exchange of the biggest gun and ammunition, it seems no evil against whomever is not a part of the bargain."

"The workplaces, including offices, business centers, and schools were shut down everywhere as people hoped for the quick resolution of the madness that was spreading all over the land. Such a hope receded day by day until a decade was not enough to stop it," she said.

As the land disintegrated into protracted anarchy, Latto became angrier about the ailing wisdom of the leaders. She had seen the destroyers becoming powerful day by day, taking over the national leadership, making the national currency and the natural resources valueless.

"The entire nation was out of the basic foods and commodities. Most people began to eat wild roots, leaves, snails, frogs, lizards, and other living things, which were available and extremely detrimental to human consumption."

Latto continued, "Many people already had swollen stomachs and legs, and peeled skin with gruesome wounds. It was so dehumanizing to see a grown up man or woman's hair turning yellow or becoming bald from the prevailing starvation.

"In fact, as life became worthless, no man knew his potential killers. The killers had no respect for human beings. The guns and voodoo were their friend and god. A teenager could be seen, holding up to a big AK-47 assaulted rifle or RPG, looking for his enemies to loot and kill."

As Latto continued, she remembered that on one Thursday afternoon, some hungry men had gone to a nearby swamp to look for some wild food; a group of teenagers surfaced in the place and began to arrest them. She saw one of the teenagers, ordering a sick looking old man to take off his clothes and to give them to him. "He ordered the man to run for his life; if not he was going to put him to sleep, meaning, kill him," she said.

"Before the man could beg or run, the little boy chopped off his head with a cutlass. The headless man took a few steps, staggered and fell with his fresh blood running on the cemented pavement, while his head was lying on the other side, gasping. Then, these children fought over his clothes as they ran from the scene, avoiding any restriction from any superior officer who might come there."

Seeing the children having no remorse, Latto wondered why the good Lord should allow such evil people to destroy innocent lives and properties. In her mind he decided that no one can actually understand the meaning of life.

Latto had seen the few men who were somehow safe, hiding, while most of their women carefully went out to collect any crumb of food for their respective families. It was so appalling for the men to see their women becoming the breadwinners. General Mullah and his armed gang could only humiliate the women, but not readily kill them as they did to the men.

Some women's hearts grieved over the mandatory house-arrest of their men and husbands. Others found it as an opportunity to disrespect their husbands or to engage in various kinds of devious lifestyles prostitution, being private detectives, rogues, or to join the bunch of criminals.

"For instance, Lesilee, a twelve-year-old girl, was kidnapped by one of the gangsters and carried deep into the war front. The next time Lesilee's parents saw her, yet still alive, was after many years having been abandoned with a number of children, sickened and poorly cared for.

"In the case of Banta, it was somehow different. As a beautiful young and married woman, she constantly went out with the armed gangsters, spending much time with them, even in trenches at the frontlines before coming home." Latto said, "Banta's husband had no say or the power to do anything. At least, his children were constantly fed. What he could not see, he did not bother to know about it. He always considered Banta as his wife, even though he did not want her to die in this lifestyle.

"Banta's husband had seen General Mullah's gang kill a lady, because she had refused to follow them. Her husband could not give her a decent burial. He lamented for the embarrassing situation and blamed General Mullah for everything."

Latto noticed that based on the evil acts of the leaders of Leewah, the land had experienced a worldwide hatred. "For instance, she remembered that one of the main causes of the hatred for Chief Doudiah started when he ordered the shooting of the dozens of elite statesmen and their relatives after taking over the state's affairs, even though most international leaders and advocacy groups had advised him not to do it. It was Doudiah, becoming the first indigenous leader, who carried on the dreadful murder; publicly executing human beings like roosters was extremely absurd. Most of the executed victims were descendents of the pioneering fathers and mothers of the land."

When Latto was growing up, she heard some beautiful stories about the elite people. For instance, she had learned that whenever there were insufficient funds to run the government of Leewah, the elite people loaned money to the nation. "In fact, the majority of them helped by creating jobs and providing scholarships for people," she said. "Since they knew international people or had shares in international businesses, they made things somehow better in the nation than it was in most third world countries. Many breadwinners came to the land and took as much substance as they could from the nation. No one bothered them. Some even used Leewah as their stepping stone to connect themselves to other countries. With aggression the unseasoned lads seized the unimaginable opportunity; they had more on their political plates to eat, enough to waste them. "

Latto regrettably said, "It could have been better for us to remain under Rev. Billy Ray and his elite people than to have come under this criminal, Chief Doudiah and his illiterate hooligans. By now, this land could have been developed. While most countries within the sub-region were yet to think about massive development, Rev. Billy Ray had already started the construction of farm-to-market roads, building schools and medical institutions, seeking and providing local and foreign scholarships, setting up the mechanism to produce more food and cash crops, and involving more indigenous sons and daughters in the national leadership. Every year, Rev. Billy Ray made a developmental slogan as a way of empowering his countrymen and women. I won't forget the popular ones like: 'Total Involvement for Higher Heights; I Will Build Thee a Great Nation; Let's Fight the War against Ignorance, Disease and Poverty; Let's Go Back to the Soil and Grow more Food; and This is Rally Time.' Since his death, every decade the nation continues to go beyond it's year of establishment. He was the first leader to have allowed a multiparty system after years of its absence in the nation. He wanted his government to be equated to other democratic governments around the world. He became the innocent victim of circumstance for the sins of most of his predecessors in the nation became his ultimate end.

"The hatred worsened, when Chief Doudiah declared the remaining pioneers illegal in Leewah," Latto stated. "The remnant pioneers had no other alternative but to flee for safety. It was believed that the pioneers in the Diasporas planned in nine years to come back and stage the greatest revenge against Doudiah's leadership. They passed through the most affected people and region in the nation to achieve their desires.

"After a long period of absence from Leewah, General Mullah had been hired, sponsored, trained and reappeared, announcing himself as the real lion of the nation." Latto said angrily, "Is he a lion for this land? Who made him a lion for us? Maybe, he meant that he has come as a lion to kill us. He has refused to admit the fact that he has come to revenge the death of Rev. Billy Ray and the elite people Chief Doudiah brutally murdered. He failed to know that pressing down Doudiah, means pressing down the entire suffering natives along with the elites.

"Just like the way I did not welcome the toppling of Rev. Billy Ray, I say again, it would be better for us to remain under the tyrannical leadership of Chief Doudiah than welcoming a leader we don't know. General Mullah may try to convince us with his numerous styles of rhetoric. Rhetoric is the known game-formula of politics, but not the reality for a purposeful development. Anybody who wants to be our new leader must not rig the system. He must start by doing some sort of development in the nation and be duly elected by the people of the land rather than having thousands of guns to force his way into our highest office. If Chief Doudiah used guns to get to power, that should not mean that every other person should do it.

"There should be a law that stops members of armed gangs, who have done atrocities, from becoming leaders of the people. We must have our land clothed with instituted laws, but not just a nation of men."

Latto described General Mullah as the unpatriotic beast and agent of the devil who is breathing his snares of death among innocent people. "He is destroying our opportunities within the land and out in the international community as well."

Latto became furious when she and the people of the world heard General Mullah address Leewah. "I have seen the suffering of the indigenous people of this nation. I have seen how Chief Doudiah is killing innocent people. I have seen how he is disrespecting our mother-nation. He has lost our credibility and confidentiality with countries within our sub-region. I cannot allow this carnage to go on unpunished. I'm going to remove Chief Doudiah along with his loyalists from this land like a bed-bug."

Latto said, "Since that Christmas Eve, General Mullah called men, women, boys and girls from all parts of the land to be members of his gang, looting, raping, and killing, he finally entered the capital as his last resort without having the remorse that the peninsula city was a refuge, having thousands of national and international people."

"It had come to be known as the legacy of Famatta. No matter how she redresses it, once such a galling utterance was heard, the people have their own way of interpreting it, because what we say or do lives after us," said Latto as she lamented for Famatta. She had seen Famatta, a well-known lady, who had been targeted several times politically, beaten, jailed and traumatized by Chief Doudiah. She became one of the strongest supporters of General Mullah during the height of his widespread destruction.

She said that Famatta voiced her feelings. "General Mullah, how long will it take to complete this struggle against Doudiah? I don't want you to be like General Bonan who came to deliver us from Chief Doudiah a few days after announcing the results of a rigged election. General Bonan failed to understand that liberation means risk-taking. He came with a biblical philosophy under his tongue, (don't shed innocent blood), that philosophy failed him. He missed Chief Doudiah. Then, Chief Doudiah ferociously killed him along with most of his followers, including journalists and a host of innocent people during his November raid in the nation."

Latto said that Famatta emphasized her point to General Mullah, "Be serious! Tell me and the people of Leewah. How long will it take you to quiet the voice of Doudiah? You know, we came for this purpose. We must be serious about what we have come to do. We are putting our reputations on the line before our people and before the world leaders. We must uphold the promise we had made to them, General Mullah."

She said, "General Mullah then answered Famatta, 'Don't worry, Ma'am. Within a matter of days, Chief Doudiah and his loyalists will be brushed out of this land like a man removing dirt from his cushions.

"Famatta ordered, 'then, go ahead and level everything until our aim is accomplished. If it is just a matter of days, we will rebuild whatever you destroy within the twinkling of an eye. Enough is enough. All that we want is Chief Doudiah. He must go in order for us to come back to clean up the mess he is depositing around here.'"

Latto believed that perhaps it was the frustration that led Famatta, a woman who seemed to have Leewah at heart, to conform herself to the wishes of a notorious man like General Mullah. It seemed that almost every single person of the land had taken a side, especially against Doudiah, without taking into consideration the consequences that would follow. The patriotic ones wondered, "Where will the funds come from? Will it come through magic, from persuaders of the war, from international nations, from Famatta or General Mullah's pocket to rebuild this shattered nation?"

Receiving assurance from Famatta and other supporters, Latto said that General Mullah once again forcefully drafted most men and women to join him to press on with his objectives. She heard him making a promise to all his fighters that they may possess as their bona fide property whatever they capture during the unrest.

"Soon, General Mullah recruited more members to his gang," Latto revealed, "The genocide intensified as they captured cars, lands, and houses, inscribing their names on them as their properties and kidnapping women and girls as their sexual objects.

"The news had spread like a blazing fire on one Friday morning. "Elder Akko, a successful businessman along with his wife and his seven children became another unforgettable victim of the unrest. When four men of General Mullah's gang entered Elder Akko's compound, they first met his adopted daughter. Each of the men raped her, while they locked up the other family members indoors.

"Thereafter, the gangsters brought out and lined up the entire family and began to kill them one by one until the nine persons were completely dead, despite their previous assurance that they were going to free them after raping the little girl," Latto said.

"Being militarily trained in the west, Captain Jerma, the nephew of Dr. Kiamu, who was caught up by the unrest, had failed to understand as he was educated in the West. He said, 'you can't put out a fire with gasoline. The people should have used the democratic process to elect effective people to run the nation. See how the nation has become the biggest undeveloped village of the world.'"

Latto asked Capt Jerma, "Democracy? What do you mean by democracy in this place, my man? Do these corrupt people know what democracy is?" We have the desire to imitate the westerners who have spent numerous centuries developing themselves and their land with a uniformed political system. The acts of corporal greed and corruption always erase the word democracy from the mind of everyone who becomes the leader of Leewah, no matter what foreign education they might have achieved."

In a similar way, Latto said that Gbormee, an elderly man who had lost his only son during the university raid, rebuked his brother who was celebrating the coming of General Mullah with his war. She said, "The man told his brother, 'General Mullah and his followers are a group of insane novices. They don't have love for this land. They have found it as a breeding place for their evils. They take this land to be their gold field. They come to tap the raw materials.'"

Latto said that Gbormee asked his brother again, "Who told you that General Mullah and his group were freedom fighters? They are unpatriotic liars. You must believe this today and to live with it."

She said, "My father always says, 'whatever you stress to its limit, it either breaks or hits back at you.'"

Latto heard Gbormee challenge General Mullah and his gang, "Let them come! We are all going to get into it. We shall know the man among us. It has been a long time since the days of our ancestors. Leewah has been dictated by all kinds of silly armed gangs. They had robbed even the sands from our ground. They have devised the medium of segregation, tribalism, nepotism and favoritism among the citizenry. They have made us illiterate people and the least developed region of the world. We must stand to say enough is enough. We must say that we need no new dynasty or czar. We must resist General Mullah."

She said, "Gbormee continued, 'we need no intervention at this time. If we owe anybody anything, we must pay it. We need no outside help. No other nation can put its nose in another nation's sovereignty.' Everybody, including international leaders heard this old man's rambling voice. Was that the will of the nation? Those who loved wars supported his utterances, while the law-abiding people continued to suffer."

Dr. Kiamu, who had been traumatized by the war, commented, "That's life. We will survive it. There was a time the Atlantic Ocean was the only outlet for those who survived to move out.

"The last plane had finally gone with those who had the opportunity to go. The fisherman boats and ships had all gone in deep seas.

"We saw those rich guys who always had their passports and tickets leaving the land, while those who did not support the unrest remained to suffer with their families."

Dr. Kiamu rested his elbow on a bench and said, "I will not expect my grandchildren to understand why I stayed to suffer. In the first place no one understands war. I must let them know that God made me to remain alive that must be the fact they should understand."

"I don't blame you, Daddy," Latto said. "My Mom was always encouraging you, 'let's watch the daily development to see what will be the outcome' as we were glued to our television, later to our radio set."

Dr. Kiamu said, "I can't blame my wife. The war traumatized everybody. I can remember on one Thursday night, I was so frustrated about what was going on that, I began to hallucinate as I talked aloud unknowingly.

"My wife was surprised to see me in such an unusual state of mind. She came in and said, 'Daddy, stop the shouting before these deadly insane bastards come around here.'

"I said, 'you are right I'm just crushed down with frustration. Why must we close one eye every night while we open the other to guard us? Why must we be glued to the radio set to hear awful news of the day about our land?'"

"As Mommy and Daddy were talking that night, I worried about my birth-mother," Latto explained. "We had just heard about the gruesome murder of her brother, Myron and her uncle, Gorto a day ago. The gangsters had slashed off their jaws and left them, bleeding in their sugar cane plantation. They thought those poor farmers had much money that they had refused to give to them."

"That was so much terrible, a terrible thing to talk about."

"Even more than terrible," Dr. Kiamu said. "When Chief Doudiah noticed that the gangsters had dressed like crazy people to enter the city, he ordered his loyalists, 'kill any crazy man. Whether you call him handicapped or disabled man, when he is found on the street kill him. No disabled person is allowed to be on the street. Those who are on the street are gangsters. They are pretending to be crazy people. Everyone knows that General

Mullah was sent by someone; somewhere who does not like my leadership to fight me. They are envious because they are watching me develop the land they thought they could continue to haul resources from.'"

Latto added, "In less than a day, Doudiah's loyalists killed almost all of the wandering disabled people in the city. During that same time, my friend Tewah was among over six hundred mothers and their children who sheltered in a church. They were slaughtered at night during a downpour of rain.

"Thereafter in another incidence, General Mullah killed hundreds of civilians, nuns, foreign journalists, and even some liberators in the suburb of the capital for lashing against his movement. Prominent leaders of the world church supported some local prominent leaders as a means to move General Mullah out of the city. General Mullah always aborted these efforts.

"In the day, there were bodies without heads or limbs, lying in the streets or in public places. A person's stomach could boil like there was a certain bowel movement ongoing in it. You could wish to go to the restroom, but there was nothing in the stomach to pass out. You could wish to drink, but water couldn't quench anyone's thirst. You could wish to call on your strongest persons to help; none had the strength and power to help you. You could run, but no place to hide. You could wish to remain where you are, but all around you wasn't safe. Your loved ones, your children, your wife, looked at you to take the last decision, while others were already on the move. No voice and power you had to take the decision. Many times, you would pray and call upon God; your wishes were not answered as you thought. It was the fear for safety, and the fear of guilt that paralyzed us. How could we see our loved ones dying, or being raped, and have no means to help them? Such a broken heart killed many people."

Latto said that during one evening, a public drinking well in the Central Province was filled with over two hundred precious children alive from the eastern region. She said that even though no one was there to claim any responsibility for the horrible deaths of those children, every finger pointed to General Mullah and his gang.

"Even my friend, Dr. Fromo, who became the president of the public university, was murdered during that same night because he had been appointed by Chief Doudiah," Dr. Kiamu lamented. "Dr. Fromo and I had graduated the same year, and we had come to Leewah at the same time to work for our government and people. How could such illiterate bastards destroy such a valuable man? Do they know how long it took to build up such a man? Like many other valuable people who had succumbed to their violent bloodbath, where will we get Dr. Fromo's replacement in this land?"

Dr. Kiamu went on to say, "One of the strangest things that happened in the war was when a person had a colonial name, that person became a target for General Mullah. Yet, a person who had a certain native name, Chief Doudiah also targeted, intending to make the vultures or dogs devour his flesh.

"The land was evenly divided on tribal lines. No one dared to venture into an unknown area unless he longed for his death. Most wives or husbands even betrayed each other to any enemy force if both of them didn't come from the same tribal land. You can imagine some children even delivered their parents either to General Mullah or to Chief Doudiah. No one was there to reprimand them."

Dr. Kiamu could not forget that day. "It was on one Tuesday night, when General Mullah and his gang entered the city," he said. "The next day, General Mullah finally declared himself as the leader of Leewah over a little private broadcasting station. He promised 'I'm going to bring you peace and prosperity. I will combat corruption. I'm going to build you paved roads from the west to the east, from the north to the south. Every city will be built to an international standard. Every citizen will be educated at every level. I will restore all the essential facilities that were destroyed during the period of our malady. I will eradicate tribalism along with those who practice it. I will bring Chief Doudiah to justice for all the crimes he has committed against the innocent.'

"When the international liberators heard his lousy rhetoric, they said, 'we thought General Mullah was fighting for the right cause. Since he wants to be like Doudiah, we will make things difficult for him.'

"That was the start of another new beginning of the struggle. Most supporters of General Mullah withdrew their alliances. General Mullah was watched and chased by many planes day and night. Splintered groups emerged every day, opposing General Mullah's objectives.

"Even though Chief Doudiah had placed himself under house-arrest with some loyal followers and family members, surrounded by opposition groups, he was still receiving support, while the humanitarian people persuaded him to leave the nation. He could not find reasons to do so. His death squad relentlessly continued his objectives."

"Our best day was when we heard that the international liberators had responded to the request of the citizens of Leewah," Latto said. "They had appealed to Chief Doudiah to relinquish his position for the sake of his people. The international liberators gave him along with a number of his followers and relatives a safe haven in any land, city or nation of his choice.

"It was the day Chief Doudiah defied the offer with his usual rhetoric, 'How can I give my land to a thief like General Mullah? He has returned as a destroyer. How can I allow a criminal who once took the people's resource to lead? We will battle it out until all of us die together.'

"His senior assistant rebuked him, 'we all weren't born together, and we all aren't going to die together.' Chief Doudiah roared at him, 'you shouldn't be a coward. You dare to say it again!' He gave his assistant a back palm clap, and all the people in the meeting heard the terrifying sound.

"Attendants of the meeting said, 'since Chief Doudiah is after destruction, he will sit in a lonely chamber and regret the opportunity he has missed.'"

Latto continued. "For some time, we had been indoors, deep in our hidden place for a week without food and water. Since there seemed to be a Momentary calm, my dad ventured outside to find some food for the family. I followed him. Our eyes caught the scene of some young men who had just burglarized the supermarket adjacent to our house.

"One of men intended to run with the bag containing some important item, perhaps money. One of them quickly passed in front of him and said, 'What do you think you are doing?' The man stood up and placed himself in a firing position with his AK-47 and asked his friend, too. 'What do you think I want to do?'"

She stated that another robber said, "I bet you with my life, if you attempt to run with that bag, only your dead body will tell the rest of your story to the world."

Latto went on, "His friend asked him, 'What will you do?'

"He said, 'kill you like a fly, you silly chap!'"

"The one who was running said, 'When you kill me I will kill you too.'

"The other man giggled and said, 'That's why I said you are a fool.'

"He then asked him, 'how will you kill me when I had already killed you?'

"He challenged the man by saying, 'okay, go ahead if that is a salt to put your tongue on, you will know whether it is sweet or spicy. You will see what I'm going to do.' He began to run from the scene. Right away, the one with the gun shot him in the back, and he fell over the bag. From the left side of the building, a third person surfaced and shot the one who had killed the first person. He came and pushed both bodies aside and took the bag away, chuckling without the least fear that what they had done was wrong."

Chapter 16

Latto remembered that August 24 could have been a nice day like any of the ones celebrated in recent years in Leewah had it not been the intransigent behaviors of General Mullah and his gang. But the day instead turned out to be the celebration of angry gunfire in the land. After many months of a merciless deathwatch, a warship released bullets from the Atlantic Ocean throughout the day, announcing the arrival of the long-awaited liberators.

As Latto explained her dilemma, she said that General Mullah fearlessly sprayed rocket-propelled grenades, missiles, and other bullets toward the liberators' ship. "At the same time, Chief Doudiah continued his killing show unabated on the other side of the city. The various opposition gangs did similar things. The civilians were caught in the middle of the many warlords, prohibiting any man being able to escape."

Latto said, "The liberators had come not as gangsters. They were under a strict mandate that they had the right to self-defense, and when gross abuse of human rights was at hand, they must intervene. They were vigilant every second.

"Within a few days after the arrival of the liberators, during one rainy Sunday in September, Chief Doudiah was finally placed in his terminal grave."

Latto remembered that morning Chief Doudiah informed the liberators from his protected palace, "I'm ready to leave now to wherever you want me to go."

And, the go-ahead was given to him.

"Without a delay, Chief Doudiah was en-route along with a handful of loyalists and tribesmen, waving to group of war-wearied citizens who had lined up on both sides of the main boulevard to catch a glimpse of their stubborn leader for the last time. His motorcade faded from the bystanders' eyes as he entered the compound of the liberators at the western outskirt of the city. Suddenly, a breakaway loyalist of General Mullah entered the compound. He informed Doudiah, 'this is my terrain. How can you pass through it without getting my permission?' He arrested Doudiah, then dragged, and butchered him. Executing a national leader of sort, no sound person in his right mind could have ever thought about doing it, instead justice prevailed."

Latto said, "After nine months of anarchy, the main target was finally down, still there was no end to the struggle as the world's political czars had expected. The response was a counteraction from the remnant group of people loyal to Chief Doudiah, parading everywhere. There was vigorous chanting heard everywhere, 'If we don't receive the living body of Chief Doudiah, there would be no more Leewah; no human beings shall remain in this place. We will revenge his death with every drop of our blood.'

"Chief Doudiah's loyalists burned houses, looted, raped, and killed hundreds of liberators along with innocent people. They finally organized themselves into another opposition armed gang. Even though the liberators and other international leaders were not happy about the death of Chief Doudiah, they hoped such an event was the end of the conflict."

Latto spoke again, "As the fighting intensified from every angle, General Mullah, too, continued to challenge the liberators. The liberators pursued him up to the Central Province of Leewah with the hope that within the next few weeks, he would be driven out of the entire region.

"The temporary governor, who had been placed in the nation's office after the death of Chief Doudiah to minister the affairs until the dispute was settled, again carried on his usual sugarcoated talks. 'Honorable liberators, please limit your raid on General Mullah for the sake of the innocent. See how you are destroying the land and the important resources with your many air-raids? It is not General Mullah you are killing, but the innocent people. We want to still have some people alive after this madness. I encourage you to seek dialogue with General Mullah. I repeat, you can't mind the ugliness of the baboon and beat it to his grave. You shouldn't mind him and kill all the people you had come to protect.'"

Latto said, "So, his voice was heard and the liberators for some weeks played the lay-low game with lives and properties.

"Since there was a window of opportunity for General Mullah, he recruited, and trained more gangsters to build up his gang, collecting more resources and later took his cause nationwide.

"Many people found it difficult to figure out the purpose of the temporary governor limiting the strength of the peacemakers against General Mullah."

"Some sort of sinister arrangement must be going on in this war," one wise thinker observed. "This land whose length from east to west can take a man less than twenty hours to cross, I see no reason why these gallant liberators can't chase out General

Mullah within a day or two; especially when General Mullah has taken a few days to reach its main capital."

The observing thinker revealed that the rumors were spreading like a savannah fire, announcing that there was some sort of evil deed going on between the temporary governor and General Mullah. "A famous communicator lost his life for saying, 'it seems like they have divided the leadership of Leewah into two parts for their selfish aims, while playing games with innocent people's lives."

Latto's mother, Leemu, watched her friends and their families, leaving Leewah. She encouraged her husband that they could not continue to stay with the children, while others are leaving every day. "This war isn't going to end now. If we don't make a move, these crooks will kill us, too," she said.

"I have told you that during war, one needs to be very wise before leaving his or her safe zone. Many people died untimely from making the wrong decision by moving from their comfort zones. Whenever we decide to move, then we must go; maybe it is the voice of a certain elder speaking to us," Dr. Kiamu said.

Latto's father utilized one idea. He walked down to his family in the basement and said, "We are about to leave this place any time.

"I have prepared a rhyme from the Bible to be our guide." As he handed them a copy, he said, "Please memorize it so that you can recite it, while we are in our hiding place." Latto's father then recited the poem:

A thousand may fall at my side,
And ten thousand at my right hand;
But none shall come near me,
'Cause my Lord is there for me.

I will fear no evil nor will I be dismayed,
He'll strengthen me in my trouble;
Yes, He'll lay me by the stilled water,
'Cause my Lord is there for me.

He'll uphold me with His righteous hand,
He'll lead me to the paths of comfort rest;
He'll make my darkness bright before me,
'Cause my Lord is there for me.
He'll be with me when I pass through the waters
He'll be with me when I walk through the fire,
He'll supply all of my needs in my days of fire.
'Cause my Lord is there for me.

"Looking at her parents," Latto said, "Even though my father was frustrated, I could still see the amazing love in his eyes when he handed us a copy of the poem and went to the left side of the basement where our mother was sitting. He couldn't do anything, but to assure us that he was still a concerned father, despite the many challenges from the gangs."

Chapter 17

Latto and her brother and the sister sat on the back porch, reciting the poem their father had shown them. They saw two men approach their house. They heard one of the men murmur "I think this is the house of Dr. Kiamu. Is there anybody in this house? Come out come out! We are here for you! I know Dr. Kiamu, you are hiding somewhere in this house. Come out, we haven't come to harm you. We have come to protect you."

Latto revealed that without hearing a response, they kicked in the back door. "They went to the front door and kicked it again," she said. "The doors came out of their hooks. They broke the glass, the bars on the windows in the living room. They finally entered the house. They turned the furniture and every other thing in the house upside down. They pointed their AK-47 assaulted rifles everywhere."

Latto continued, "Again, one of the assailants said, 'I give you the last call. We know this is your house, Dr. Kiamu. Please come out! We have come for you and your family! Don't be afraid!' The men continued yelling, knocking, and kicking any part of the house, searching for the family."

While these men were shouting, the children had carefully sneaked in and joined their parents in their hideout. "We are finished. Those are the gangsters," whispered Manu to her parents. "I know you are hearing the landowners, our killers upstairs."

"We are not finished, Babygirl. They are not our killers," answered Dr. Kiamu in a whisper. "I'm going upstairs. Man dies only once, and his news only stays around for seven days and seven nights, thereafter nobody thinks about him again. I can't stay alive while somebody comes to destroy my family without making one last attempt." Dr. Kiamu turned around to his wife and said, "Darling, take care of the children in case anything happens to me."

"I'm not taking care of your children. You aren't going to die. You have already lost your bosom friend, Dr. Fromo. I will not let you gamble with your life. I don't want you to take one step up there!"

"I don't have a choice," Dr. Kiamu insisted. "I'm already on my way to them. Let them kill me."

"How can you go to them when you know that they are heartless goons? Don't gamble with your life with those killers. Let us watch carefully," Leemu pleaded with her husband, who was missing his steps because of fear as he continued to climb upstairs.

"How can I stay here and let those sons of the devil destroy you? Then, why did you marry me? Was it not also for me to protect you and our children? Upon my dead body such a thing will happen to my family."

"Not your dead body at this time! Daddy, I know you love us. This is not the way to show your love by giving yourself to these assailants," Leemu said.

"I don't think they are our assailants. In fact, somebody among them seems to know us." Dr. Kiamu turned and looked at his wife, feeling a bit relieved from the fear.

"My dear, I thought you knew the tricks of these notorious criminals? No animal will harm human beings but human beings," Leemu said. "Calling your name shouldn't make you brave to climb into your deathtrap with those swine, honey."

"Well, let it be your truth," said Dr. Kiamu, neglecting to listen to the voice of his wife as he climbed upstairs and asked. "Who is that calling me? Who are you? Here is your doctor."

"We are your saviors," answered the two young men with red clothes tied on their foreheads, and their guns prepared to even kill a fly. "We are former students of this nursing school. Don't be afraid of us. We are just part of the struggle to liberate our land from political criminals. We mean no harm to any law-abiding citizen. The enemies of the land are the people we are after to destroy them before they destroy us."

Dr. Kiamu quickly thanked and asked them to have seat.

One of the so-called saviors said, "We have no time to wait. We have come to carry you and your family to a better place. This place is no longer safe. Those gangsters are all around here."

One of the assailants continued. "Within the next few hours, they are going to ransack everywhere, looking for wealth. They are used to eating human being's hearts and lungs for their medicine. They are ruthless and fearless criminals. They have promised to burn down this hospital. We want to carry you away before some wicked people come and destroy you. You mean a lot to this land.

"After all, when this insanity is over, people like you will be needed to restructure our senses. Look, we only need two hundred dollars from each of you. If you want to live, don't utter any word of excuse."

"No, take your time with the professor," the other crook rebuked his colleague.

"Look, are we here to delay? Why must you resist my command? Don't you think I care for my life, too? So, let them make haste and pack their belongings. Get few things and put them in our car. Those guys are already here."

"Get our money from them first!" the other assailant reminded his friend.

Leemu, who had stood behind her husband, whispered to him, "I am convinced! They are the real saviors we have been wishing for. I recognize both of them as I taught them last year. Let's do what they say and get out of here. For days, we have been out of food. Going to a safe land means that my children will find something good to eat."

"The way I look at these boys, they are our assailants. You don't think former students can't be wicked in some manner to their former instructor" asked Dr. Kiamu. "Prayer is the most important task we must engage in."

"We know these guys, they won't be that wicked to us, honey. Leave everything with God. Give them the money and let us move from here," Leemu said.

"No! There is no mercy in a cobra's mouth for a frog, but to slash and gulp it. I don't think there is pity in the voices of these blood-thirsty snippy boys, either," Dr. Kiamu whispered to his wife. "Anyway this isn't the time for a long argument. But I still don't trust them."

"Well, you don't have to take a risk, "said Leemu. "If that's the only alternative, we must trust in the Lord and risk our lives.

In wars any decision to protect a life always comes from a divine being."

While Dr. Kiamu and his wife were deciding on what to do, one of the assailants interrupted them. "We have no time. Let's go. The other guys will soon burn this place down. There is no time to waste." Hurriedly, they left the place.

At the outskirt of the compound, one of the assailants, said, "Stop the car!" He got out of the car and began to go back to the compound. "I'm staying here to protect your house, doctor. You and your family go with my friend. Don't worry. I will also lock everything, including the poultry. I will protect them."

"Don't worry about anything," the other assailant encouraged us as he drove from the scene and led the Kiamus to the northeastern part (the area where the war started from).

"Everything will be just fine around here," the assailant giggled, palming the wheel of the jeep, which they had intentionally cut off the top to match up with their deeds.

"I worry about our belongings," Leemu whispered to her husband.

"Honey, let's think about where are carrying the children. There is no time for that now!"

Seeing the fright in her face, the criminal asked, "Is she still worrying about her things? Your life or your things, which one do you need? You are still thinking about that junk? You better pray that I still have my right mind to carry you to safety."

As the lady continued to whisper to her husband because of the stress she was feeling, their assailant twirled the car around to the direction they just came from and asked. "Who is the lady that is still talking in this car?" He turned to look at Leemu as a way of intimidating her. "Do you want your flesh in the mouths of those bloodthirsty gangsters?"

"Well, my child, let's proceed. This is your time," Leemu said.

"Are you still challenging me?" the assailant asked as he stood over Leemu, looking on the other side at Dr. Kiamu. "I thought you were going to say something. I was going to carry you back. Let the gangsters eat some of your flesh today.

"When you crow, no other rooster can crow in the same basket," Leemu said. "Don't mind what had happened. Please do the right thing since you have decided to protect my family."

"Now you have come to your senses?" the hooligan giggled.

"Oh, how I can't recollect my wearied sense?" Leemu said. "You are our savior as you say. Who can challenge you?"

"Well, I can see your problem, your fear. Everything will be fine." The crook got back in the car and drove it in an unknown direction.

"All that I know, wherever we go we are going to get some new things." Dr. Kiamu stated as he whispered to her. "In wars, you can't own anything. The only thing you can fight for is your life. The rest of the things belong to the armed gangs."

By night, they had reached the River Jackson, which serves as the boundary between the central and the northeastern provinces.

The place was oozing with fear. The gangsters had killed many people and improperly buried some. Some bodies were still lying everywhere. The armed gang had decorated their various gates with human skulls and intestines. A garrison of flies was roaming the area, depositing billions of their young ones everywhere.

The assailant who was driving the Kiamus got out of the jeep and looking at the area, said, "No fighter knows his people during wars. We have raped women, young girls, including our own sisters, our mothers, and our aunts.

"In fact, any woman or man was our wife. We did any thing to make our medicine strong against our enemies. We humiliated the stubborn men and women in any way we thought to satisfy our desires."

The assailant looked around to make sure that no other gangsters were there and said, "That's the first thing we are instructed to do before our master can know that we are serious.

"When we came, we threw countless number of escapees into this river. If this river could say, 'I'm full,' then it would have stopped us from dumping people into it."

The assailant continued to frighten them and laughed foolishly about it. "You know, human beings' blood, the heart, and the lungs are also good for our medicines. In fact, we ate them daily as our meals, which were a kind of fun."

Dr. Kiamu again became very critical about the man who was transporting them. He came to the conclusion that the man was their main assailant instead of being their savior. He lamented, "How people who were created by God could be so wicked to others like a gorilla? I hope the Lord won't allow this fool to think about doing anything foolish tonight. I would show him that I'm also a man. I cannot let this single man, a man who is less than five feet destroy the family of a six foot man like me."

When Manu and Latto saw that Numeh was frightened, they too put their fingers into their ears. They didn't want to hear such a fearful story anymore.

The assailant told them that the Jeep was out of gasoline. He said, "It will be better for us to spend the night in this village. In the morning, I will go to a nearby town to look for gasoline."

Hearing the assailant make this kind of useless statement, Dr. Kiamu wondered about this young man with him. His heart was heavy.

Dr. Kiamu asked himself, "Where will this guy get gasoline in this forest? Since we have been traveling, we haven't seen any live village. Gangsters have burned all the villages and towns."

When the man noticed the fright in Dr. Kiamu's eyes, he marveled they had actually become his victims for the night.

The assailant said, "Don't be afraid; nobody will bother us here. This isn't the route that any fighter would like to take, especially in the night. I have been in this business for many months. We were the first people General Mullah recruited. We have done anything we could. I am tired of doing wickedness. This is one of the reasons you see me, looking for a way to save others. Do not worry. I know where we will pass. I have been carrying people across this river many times for little or nothing. Why I can't do the same thing for my own people."

"Hmm, are you a Kpelle?"

"Yeah!"

“From where?” the fearing Leemu asked the assailant.

“My mother is a Kpelle woman, and my father is a Mano man from a village somewhere down this river. I basically grew up along this river. So, do not worry.”

Looking at the Kiamus, the criminal bragged, “War is the equalizer. It has made every man equal. Those who couldn’t wear a nice looking a pair of trousers or shirts are now the kings because they are making use of the killer weapons against the weak. Many of our friends who refused to make use of a simple logic are all dead today. I always make sure that I select the best route for my survival and for you whom I’m carrying.”

Latto and her parents entered one emptied building with no front and back doors and left the man outside along with the jeep and their few belongings.

“I will sleep in the Jeep to protect your things and to keep a watch for any intruder,” the assailant decided.

The Kiamu family couldn’t sleep. They couldn’t trust their so-called savior. Finally, the moonlight that served as the only source of light had gone beyond the forest. The big trees along the riverbank darkened the village. The birds and other animals had stopped their swaggering sounds. The roaring tide from the river had carried the Kiamus to their unexpected sleep.

The assailant who called himself a savior, when he noticed that Dr. Kiamu and his family were asleep was happy. He quickly rolled the jeep on to the tiny motor road. He drove it back to the hospital compound, where he had earlier take Dr. Kiamu and his family from, joining his friend who remained there.

Chapter 18

Latto and her family woke up to the chirping of the forest birds. They couldn't believe that they had ever slept in such a stinky house with its messy surroundings.

Dr. Kiamu hopped into the empty doorway. To his surprise, the bright sunlight made him aware that it was another terrifying day. He looked and looked. Nowhere could their so-called savior be found.

"We are finished, Darling," he shouted. "The son of the devil has run away with our little belongings. I knew those crooks were our assailants. I knew, I knew…"

"Calm down. Control your voice. Who didn't know this could happen?" Leemu said. "All along I have expected this kind of thing to happen to us. That was why I continued to argue with everybody, especially with him, because I knew that he was going to be our assailant."

"You did not argue more than I did. Anyway, that is not important now. Don't blame yourself or anybody right now. We have no other alternative. We must make haste and leave this place before he comes with his reinforcements to do the dirtiest thing to us," Dr. Kiamu advised.

"Then, let's speed up and move from here," his wife agreed.

"Look, there's a note on the bamboo bench," said Manu, showing it to her parents.

As Dr. Kiamu made the attempt to take it from his daughter, Leemu asked him, "Do you want to read it? What sense will it represent? What benefit will you get from reading that rubbish?"

"My name is on it," Dr. Kiamu said.

"Your name and so what does not that mean?"

"Maybe, he's gone to buy the gasoline and he did not want to bother us from our sleep."

"And so, that is how you think now? Did you give him any money?" Leemu asked.

"No!"

"Why don't you think this assailant has planned to use his gun at us?"

"If he wanted, he could have done it a long time ago."

"He was looking for the right time. And he had found it.

"It makes no sense for him to use his own money to buy gasoline to transport us. You saw him when he hijacked money from us. In fact, where in this world, will a thief use his own money to help people he had stolen from?"

As Dr. Kiamu forced himself to read the note, he shouted, "You are right. It's a threatening note from the goon of hell. It is publicly known that he is our assailant. The note reads."

Mr. and Mrs. Educators, I think by now you already know your fate. I did well to have brought you this far. Never have you talked about coming back this way until our days are over in Leewah. I am going to join my friend to rage the hell out of things.

I don't think you want to bother yourselves about what you have left behind. In fact, what are they, a bunch of trash or junk? Well, if you venture to come, flies and vultures will feast on your flesh as you have already seen others' bodies lying in waste at this river. I don't think you will return like a fool to do that. If you did, that would be your chance to join Dr. Fromo or Chief Doudiah in the great beyond. What makes you better than those who have gone there? Find out for yourselves. Good-bye bookworms!

Dr. Kiamu exhaled, "I'm convinced that destruction comes in many ways; even through people who seem to be your own people. Trusting anybody during war should be the last thing you do."

As Dr. Kiamu and his family walked along a pathway, they didn't meet or hear any human being, except the echoes of wild animals in the forest. With an overwhelming fright, fatigue and hunger they couldn't withstand the walk. Since the children were born, they hadn't trekked such a distance or encountered such a hunger.

They refused to drink from the nearby muddy creeks, which seemed to be infested with some water-borne bacteria. Dr. Kiamu and his family had been used to drinking pipe-borne water.

Within a few hours, the family reached at the site of an abandoned sugarcane plantation. Dr. Kiamu used the little strength he had and cut some of the sugar canes.

He went to the stream and washed them up thoroughly. They chewed on them and regained some strength.

"These dried ones are good treatments for stomach wounds," Dr. Kiamu said.

"Daddy, do you know what kind of place this was?" Latto inquired.

"I knew that you would ask after you had eaten something. I must thank whosoever for this sugarcane. Latto's bag is filled, again. We are back with our team time quiz," Leemu joked.

Manu took a peel of the sugarcane and threw it at Latto. As everyone burst with laughter, Leemu said, "Remember we are still in a land of the stinky boys. Any son of the devil could be walking alongside the road. When he hears our noise, he would chase us to our death."

The place once again became quiet as they continued to tramp. Leemu's legs had swollen up, while Dr. Kiamu's legs too were peeling from the horrible walk. He had been walking without any shoes or sandals. Their assailant had carried their things, including his sandals away.

He didn't mind his condition, but wanted to care for his wife and the children. "Let's go back to traditional medicine," Dr. Kiamu said. "My grandfather once showed me some useful leaves that heal fresh wounds. He said any leaf animals eat is either a medicine or a food. It was one of the trial and error methods our ancestors used to discover what was best for their livelihood. I wish they had the knowledge to transfer their ideas to a greater number of people in our various communities or to keep them for the future."

Dr. Kiamu cut certain leaves and squeezed them in the calabash he took from the sugar cane plantation. He applied its greenish fluids on their wounds. They sat for a while as the fresh substance burned into the new wounds, healing them.

Thereafter, when they reached a camp of a rubber plantation, a heap of human bones had been placed in the middle of the village. Some of General Mullah's gangsters had burned the camp just a few months ago and killed the residents.

Leemu carried her face on other side and cried, "Why must General Mullah do this horrible thing?

These bones are the bones of our people,

The bones of statesmen and women who ruled us,

The bones of real people, not grasshoppers,

The bones of real family men and women,

The bones of precious children: our future leaders,

The bones of the ordinary people, who knew nothing about this war,

The bones of people, who had this nation at heart and supported it;

Here, they are lying in heaps of bones, having no chance to build this land.

Where will we find their replacements?

We still have a long way to go to learn and practice patriotism."

When the children too saw the bones, they cried profusely. They covered their faces with their palms and joined their parents in rushing out of the village.

It was three more days before the Kiamus managed to reach to the northeastern border of Leewah with Little France. Surprisingly, they met a family who had been intending to cross in to the nearby land of Little France.

The mother in the family said to Leemu, "Feel free to share with us. We may not have known one another before. We are now getting to know one another." The kind lady encouraged Leemu. "We are from the same nation, suffering for survival. This is not the time to play a shame game for your needs. Let the children eat with their friends." She sat a dish of fried plantain with beans and egg before the children.

"Thanks," Leemu said to the lady who had come along with her husband from overseas to relocate their parents. The lady and her husband had been at the boarder for the past two weeks. They hadn't seen any of their people. What the little money they had, they shared with the Kiamus to help them pay for a room in the hotel for the night.

"Some people are just extraordinarily good. The man and his wife are willing to help others when they are distressed, and they don't even know us," Dr. Kiamu marveled.

Before entering, Little France the next day, a man at the gate requested Dr. Kiamu to pay a certain amount of money to him as an entrance fee. He charged for every piece of bag (small or big) they were carrying. The man intimidated Dr. Kiamu before his family and said, "If you don't have money to pay, you will either go back to continue killing yourself or I will lock you up. We are not the people who brought you war. You are not to be loitering in other's people nation. You're supposed to remain in your nation to face the reality of your own consequences. Since you have money to go around the world to cause more confusion, you must pay any amount I charge you. We are people of laws. If you are coming into our land, you must dance to the tune of the music we sing."

"Well, say all what you want to say," Dr. Kiamu said to him. "I will continue to beg you for now. We are the same brothers and sisters with our countries bordering one another. Did you hear your head leader say we are one people, only the Europeans divided us? Do you know that we speak the same local dialect? Do you pretend to hide yourself behind the European language we all borrowed to speak? You may not know that we are one people, because you are blind with what you are doing to us."

The man in Little France said, "We aren't the same people. You are murderers; you are killers from a wicked land. We have no connection with you. We don't kill our people. Our people are nice. We will continue to care for our people and our nation. We are people of laws, and that's how we were born to be. We shall always remain like that, unless we allow you to infest our land with your evil way of doing things."

"Yes, you are right," said Dr. Kiamu. "When your people were plowing our land for their needs, when your nation was underdeveloped, where were you? Where were you when your people allowed gangs to come to our land to destroy us? Did you not see them? Tell me if you have not benefited from our land one way or the other, especially at this gate. Look, you have made this boundary as your gold well, exploiting our traumatized people for your unnecessary needs. Now our problem is war; yours tomorrow may be different. It may be something else some of your people will need from our nation and come there for it. We will always be nice to them. We will always show them that we are human beings. We are not angry gorillas and cruel bulls. The words of your head leader must always stand that we are all one people."

"So, are you swearing us?"

"Swear? A fact can't be a swearing, my friend. I fear God. I don't swear people. I love everybody, including you," Dr. Kiamu said. "I'm a career medical doctor; besides, I am a devout believer in the supreme God. It's only the Divine God that blesses or curses people, depending on their interactions with their fellow human beings."

"We know more people like you. And he can't curse our land. But here you are. I will let you go for now. I don't want to see you crossing here again," the man warned.

The Kiamus didn't mind the dilemma. They noted that in every society there are people who discriminate against strangers. The citizens, at least the majority of them appeared very unreceptive to strangers. Some doubled the prices of the basic commodities for strangers. They forced them to pay for all services. When the strangers collected firewood from their lands, they confiscated them. No one was dared to make a vegetable garden without the permission of the presumed owner of the land or place. They weren't used to interacting with other people.

Sometimes, most people are just extraordinarily careful. They don't want to give themselves up to people they don't know very well. It takes some time for people to get used to others or to accept other people in the real world.

The government of Little France even advised its citizens, "Treat strangers with courtesy, whether you know them or not. All human beings are the same; we are only separated by land, language, not color or race. Troubles are not a reward for a particular person or people. As for the people of Leewah, they never looked for the trouble they are encountering today. Therefore, we shouldn't take them to be refugees and place them in a camp. They will live among us. And you will accept them as your brothers and sisters. They will have the opportunity to marry our children and we will do similarly. If they want to live here forever they will have the freedom to do so," the leader said.

Three days after Dr. Kiamu and his family had crossed the corrupt border, Manu called to their father. "Daddy come and converse with your children for a while."

"Anything special?" he asked.

"Not exactly!" she answered. "You know every minute we miss you, especially since you have remained alive, Daddy."

"I tell you, my child!

"That is the nicest way to show appreciation to the Lord for what he has done for the family, especially for a man like me to survive, walking many days with women. It is a blessing. I could have been killed. You couldn't have seen your father again. Now that I'm still alive, you will have every comfort from me, children."

"You need some assistance from us, too," said Manu as she put her hand around her Daddy's shoulders while she had a certain wrapped cloth in the other hand. "Here is the change from our piggy bank. Latto and I managed to hide it and brought it along with us."

"How did you manage to hide this amount of money?" Dr. Kiamu asked his children with excitements.

"It's because we are women. We brought you men into this world. We are your mothers," Leemu bragged.

"Well, I'm very thankful. I don't want to know your secrets, ladies."

A few hours later, Dr. Kiamu rushed to a local bank and changed the money to the local currency of Little France. But he discovered that the teller had made a mistake and gave him four times the value of the money he exchanged. "I wonder this man wanted to entrap me like some people usually do to find out rogues," he thought.

He went back to the bank and informed the teller, thinking that he might have made a mistake and gave him more money or he had planned some sort of scam to have him arrested.

The teller told him, "I don't think so. Please do not bother me. I gave you the correct amount for your money." All the people who were in the queue looked at Dr. Kiamu as if to say he was coming from a different planet with different norms.

Dr. Kiamu still insisted, "I don't want to use money that doesn't belong to me."

Then the teller said, "Okay, I will check my intake; if there is a difference, then you are right."

After conducting his quick inventory of his transaction for the day, he discovered that he was short the amount of money under dispute.

The teller carried his head closer to Dr. Kiamu and said, "I'm sorry, sir. Why you seem to be so much better than others. I'm impressed to see a God-fearing man like you."

Dr. Kiamu became somehow cajoled and asked the teller, "Who are you calling others? Do you mean people from Leewah? That was one of the reasons I wanted to prove that there are still good people among us just like any other group of living beings."

The teller informed his manager about what had transpired between them. A few days later, the bank manager contacted Dr. Kiamu surprising him.

"When my teller told me about you I was impressed. I wanted to surprise you;" he said, "Please accept this little present for your family. Here is my card, call me any time when you have any problem."

Dr. Kiamu couldn't imagine which god has brightened his path on that particular day at the time when his family was out of every sundry item in the home

"As I said to your teller the other day, our nation is at war, but most of us are innocent. We are good and professional people. I wanted to use that scene to teach others that it pays to be honest, even if a person is at the threat-end of life. He must always remain faithful. Faithfulness is the formula of the long life we all wish for."

When Dr. Kiamu went home, he realized that the parcel contained much money. The amount underwrote the cost of their stay in Little France for a few more months.

The next day, Dr. Kiamu also connected himself with Dr. Selma abroad. She agreed to assist his family in any way while they were still in transit.

As Latto watched them, she asked, "Daddy, what was that little thing in your hand that looked like a turtle's shell? I saw you, laughing and talking to it."

"Oh, my little girl, have you heard the word, telephone before?"

"Nope!"

"It's one of the effective tools for modern communication."

"Communication? What do you call communication?"

"Communication is talking with other people. Back in the village, a town crier is the person that calls the villagers together to get an important message from the chief. The town crier works along with the messenger, who treks distances to deliver messages to people on the farms or in other villages. Now, telephones and other gadgets have enhanced our modern communication. We should be thankful that our brains are discovering new things everyday."

"How long does it take for the other person to receive the message through the telephone set?

"As I was talking with my friend, she received the message the same way you and I are talking and understanding one another. My friend abroad heard my own voice. I could clarify some information in my communication if she didn't understand it and I got my results from her before leaving the telephone booth. Those are the magical works you will be seeing as you travel away from your mother's fireplace, my young lady."

Latto took a long breath with a funny look. The family laughed about it.

She said, "I can't imagine anything like a telephone. I may compare that to the sand-play Jucuma had with his friends. They cut a hole in two cans and put a rope through them. They pulled the cans in the opposite directions to straighten the rope, while they talked through them to one another. They heard one another very clearly. Maybe it's from this kind of play the civilized countries developed a telephone," she thought.

They had some money and felt they could do anything. It was one of the happiest moments in months for the Kiamus.

They had gone to several places, including a local zoo, where Latto saw the giraffes, the elephants, the chimpanzees, the hippopotamus, the leopards, and the boa constrictors, jumping here and there looking for outlets to regain their freedom.

She said, "Mommy, I'm not feeling as happy as I was when we entered this compound."

"Why, Honey?"

"Is there any reason why they placed these animals in a prison compound?" Latto asked, "What have these animals done?"

"They have not done anything. This is not a prison, but a zoo."

"Why do you call this place a zoo? This place is a prison for the animals. What makes it different from a prison when the animals don't have a freedom just like the human prisoners?"

She added, "You know Mom, these animals are supposed to be enjoying the wildlife, jumping from tree to tree. Now, they are sitting here day and night waiting for someone to feed them. Don't you think that would make them aggressive and wanting to attack any human being who goes close to feed them?"

Latto had heard about some of these animals, but she hadn't seen them. A friend had, in fact, told her how a lion dismembered a man who tempted it when he entered a zoo. Latto kept her distance as far as she could to hide herself behind her mother.

"Well, Latto, what you have just said is true. We can look at the truth in a different way. These animals are less harmful than when they were in the bush. Animals are the worst carriers of many diseases. They are retained in places like this zoo for many reasons: entertainment, research, treatment, and exhibition.

"Researchers usually come to do some research on them so that they can discover diseases and find possible treatments. Also, due to the advancement of human beings, the habitats of these animals have been destroyed. Some of the animals adapt themselves to a certain temperature in their habitats before they can survive.

"Since there are no longer many lonely bushes for the animals, their generations are gradually disappearing. Like the dinosaurs, they disappeared due to the hot temperature.

"Some of the animals are kept here to protect them from wild hunters. These animals are also kept for exhibition. People like you who haven't seen them can come to see them. I didn't see a hippopotamus in the normal habitat until I came here. You would be surprised to know that there are animal hospitals and doctors. When I first visited the United States, I was surprised to see a bull-dog, wearing eye-glasses after a major eye surgery. There are also security personnel who protect them. Animal abuse is a serious crime in the white man's world."

"These are all good ideas but I don't think God planned that animals should live in cages or zoos, sitting so pitifully throughout their lives. That is the wickedest idea the higher class animals has invented against the lower class animals. I wonder if these animals will ever forgive us."

"Well, if that is how you feel, you are entitled to your opinion," Latto's mother responded.

Chapter 19

Life had become unbearable for Latto and her family in Little France again. The little amount of money they brought from Leewah plus the other money the bank manager had given them was gone. There was no job facility. Even if there was, they could not allow another national the privilege to work.

The poorly managed apartment where the Kiamus resided had no constant water supply. Privacy was not respected at the apartment during the five months they spent there.

Protecting one's life and his belongings was a personal responsibility there. For instance, when Latto and her family washed their laundry, they sat nearby to watch them as they dried, or else they were stolen. Trash and flies were everywhere. The children continued to get sick from them. They had no medical insurance. The children weren't going to school either.

Everyday they heard horrible news about their homeland. Most of the people in Little France ridiculed them. "Why can't you go to your land? You have come to enjoy our resources. You are even taking over our jobs."

One Wednesday evening, three men entered the apartment the Kiamus were renting. One of them had a gun with a rope tied to his hand. The other two also had machetes with ropes tied to their hands.

The younger man among them intended to rape one of the women in front of the children and the men. The older man halted him. "We didn't come here for that. Let's make haste, take all the valuables from these fools and leave this place." Before the Kiamus came to their senses, the three men had raided everything everywhere and left the place.

Dr. Kiamu remembered, "These men first went to a compound in the area. A lady had directed them to us, because we were strangers, and we had come with a lot of money. She informed them that she was a local person and she didn't have any money like us. The men said to her, 'we know you have your brothers and sisters abroad. They send you money regularly. That's why we have come to get our share.'

"They placed the lady along with her boyfriend in the bathroom and locked the door on them. They raided everything from them before coming to us at the next house. When Numeh saw me blocking the door in order to stop the bandits from entering, he quickly placed himself into an empty bag and forced himself among the firewood in the corner.

"When the men finally overpowered me and entered, they didn't see him. Perhaps, if the raiders meant to kill us, only Numeh could have survived because he remained unseen."

Earlier during the same evening, Dr. Kiamu learned that some armed gangsters had brutally killed some of his colleagues on the hospital compound along with important people back home. Most of the buildings in the compound and the capital city of the Central Province of Leewah were looted and burned.

Dr. Kiamu's birth's village had been burned down and most of his kinsmen killed for his sake. His uncle, who had worked as a local chief clerk, was arrested and they tore his jaws on both sides and he died from the excruciating pain. His cousin, who was the regional journalist, was also murdered. He was accused of reporting for the regional leaders and Doudiah, instead of the activity of General Mullah and his bunch of criminals.

While everyone was running from General Mullah and his forces, Dr. Kiamu's grandfather was left alone in town and later died from starvation. This was the hardest news to ever reach Dr. Kiamu. He and his family grieved for many days.

Chapter 20

Despite all the heartbreaking news from Leewah, Latto enjoyed the ocean breeze in another land. She felt secure. She saw her world open up to opportunities. She remembered her days of seeing the dead bodies of nation-builders, running from strayed bullets, living without food and water; fearing the constant intimidation and name calling by people who thought they were doing the right thing to their fellow men and women those days were over.

Even though Latto didn't fear attacks from the predators and the looters, she was always concerned about the whereabouts of her biological mother, Suah and other kinsmen who were still defenseless in Leewah. She said, "No matter what life I live, I can't easily forget them. The awful memory of the war will always ring in my ears."

As Latto and her family discussed their ugly feelings, Mona, a lady who attended school with Leemu, entered the living room. She had been displaced in Little France after the brutal killing of her husband and her five children during the civil war. She had survived because she wasn't at home on the day those goons killed her people.

Mona got Leemu's attention and said, "Have you heard about the game called diversity lottery? Most tenants in this apartment are playing it."

Leemu asked, "What kind of game is it?"

"I'm not talking about a game actually, it is a lottery," Mona corrected.

"Mona, with all the respect I have for you, I'm not thinking about anything like that for now."

"Leemu, I'm worried as much as you are. Since we are alive, we need to do something for us. One thing, life does not wait for anybody. Life always goes on no matter how many times you face grievous situations.

"My parents suffered, cutting palm nuts to underwrite the fees for my education. I thought they would have lived along with my beautiful children and my husband to enjoy my fruit," Mona said.

"However, we have to live with that. I came to tell you about a great game that enables thousands of people to travel abroad. When you win it, you will get a visa for America. Our people say, 'when you have a troublesome ailment, you seek the rigid treatments.' Since we are in need of help, we must try every opportunity. We don't know which one will benefit us."

"Huh, playing games isn't my passion. I don't have luck in it. Even common card games, I don't play them."

"It will cost you nothing to play."

"No, the fact is I don't like to put my hope into anything that has such a limited chance. It's a nice idea for some people, but I don't think I will waste my little strength going after that, Mona."

"I knew you would say that. You are always careful with all that you do," said Mona. "How much will it cost you to take a sheet to write?"

Leemu said, "I thought you were talking about a different game. Do you know how many times I have played that game? Even a friend played it for me for more than three years. Still, I couldn't win. So my luck isn't in a game. Maybe the Lord has provided my luck in many other things rather than games."

"So my friend, you still maintain your odd behavior after all these years? You are always hard to convince. Why can't you just agree with friends at times?"

"No, my friend you don't need to shout at me. I don't think it's a matter of being difficult to convince. You can't force me to be like you."

"Okay, you are right! Please let me go and worry about my problem." While exiting, she slammed the front door's screen and left the place.

Chapter 21

Latto and her family had somehow accepted themselves as refugees in Little France. They had learned to overcome the trauma day by day.

One evening, the Kiamus shared their supper. A man came in and presented a big brown envelope to Dr. Kiamu. He became very frightened and called his wife, "I have received an envelope and I don't know what it contains. Have you written anybody?"

"No! Whose name is on it?"

"Mine."

"Then, who else could have done it?" Leemu asked.

"Maybe I should return it."

"Return it? Daddy, please open it! I want to see what is inside," Numeh cried out.

As was their custom, the family quickly knelt near a sofa and prayed for fortunes rather than receiving any disturbing news, again.

Then Dr. Kiamu opened the envelope, and shouted, "What a big surprise. I can't believe it. Oh I can't believe my eyes. Honey, come and see! We have won the lottery for America."

"Then our trouble is over," Leemu answered as she staggered to stand to celebrate the joy.

"I can't imagine it. I can't believe it. What else could we want in this world? I'm thankful to the Lord for his blessings upon this family. The Lord is allowing me to travel with my family." Dr. Kiamu marveled as he gave the letter to the children so each of them could read it.

All things have been worked out. They were ready to leave.

On the day of their departure, some refugee friends gathered at the airport and celebrated with them. They hugged. They shared tears of joy with Dr. Kiamu and his family for surviving the war, unlike most of their countrymen and women who did not make it.

"Why are those people waving their hands?" Latto wondered. "Don't they want us to come back?

"Uncle Myron once told me that the way a traveler waves his hands determines the number of years he will spend on the trip. See how Daddy and Mommy are waving their hands. This means that they do not want to come back to their homeland anymore.

"As for me, I will not wave my hand because I love my people. I want to always see my mother, Suah. I will come back someday to enlighten my people," said Latto.

Each time Latto's parents talked about going to the western world, she wondered about the day she would get on a plane to fly over her village and her people. She thought about the many things she had learned about the white man's world. She had learned from Myron that rain can turn into icy particles called snow, which can remain on the ground for several weeks.

She had also learned from him that fortunes were found everywhere, money was scattered on the ground everywhere. "People work in prestigious offices with good salaries," he said. "There is no poor man. Every man is a humanitarian. They share their wealth with those who seem to have less or none."

In fact, Myron had also told Latto that whenever two persons sneezed at the same time in the white man's world, they would be paid with a good amount of money.

But she couldn't believe that reality when she also learned from her father that most of the time many people readjust their lives, learning new careers, doing dirty jobs for clean money. He told Latto, "Being abroad is a secret. You cannot narrate all you do to earn a living to your new friend or lover, but doing that is better than being in the hands of the armed gangs, where your survival is determined by them. The things you have learned will help you earn the money you need in life."

As Latto and her family were boarding the plane, her father advised her, "Latto, hold your mother's hand or come closer so that I can hold your hand. I don't want you to fall on the escalators."

"How do I walk on a running belt? Is there any other place to walk?" Latto inquired with a fright as she looked at the escalators going up and down in the hallway.

"We are entering another civilization. You will see lots of strange things. Even though there are other areas to walk, escalators are used to speedily facilitate our movement from one end of a hall to another. Some bigger airports have certain automobiles like trains that carry people around the airfield.

"You will see when the plane takes off or when it lands at

another airfield," Leemu said as she smiled with Latto. "Just build up more memories from all that you will come across each day."

Latto inquired from her father, "I watched the video screens, rolling with lots of messages. Now, I'm seeing the security, putting our luggage into a machine, then into a hole. I see them put an iron on our chests. They allow us to pass through another one. What really is security looking for?"

"Did you hear about those people who once went to our nation to destroy it? I mean the crooks who called themselves freedom fighters," said Dr. Kiamu.

"You mean General Mullah and his cruel murderers?"

"Yes!"

"Why must you talk about them here?" Leemu interrupted.

"I just want to illustrate a point."

"You don't have to go down that road with your daughter. I don't want to hear anything about those sons of the devil," Leemu said.

Dr. Kiamu said, "Let me explain my point this way. If the security does not check every passenger properly, some bad people could enter this plane to kill innocent people again. Some carry bad weapons to destroy innocent people in other land. So, every developed nation has certain equipment that detects the movement within and around their airfields."

"Then, why didn't the security check those criminals thoroughly before letting them come to our land? They came from the same developed nation, and they did not check them very well, allowing them to destroy our land and to kill our people," said Latto as she turned her face away from her Daddy. She bowed her head and wept pitifully.

"See how developed this nation is. I know it's developed because every citizen loves this nation. We are going to live in other people's land for safety. Why must we run to them, when the Lord has given all of us equal opportunities? They aren't responsible for our trouble. It's a hard thing to be away from your kinsmen whom you grew up with. You have to continue living in agony and humiliation until your death."

"My Baby, that's the question we have been looking for the answer to. We will not find the answer until the Lord himself answers it for us," her father responded as he turned to her. "The good thing is that any place can be your home. I'm happy that your mother is still alive. We will always visit her. In fact, there will be a time when she will come to visit us to see how we are living."

Latto's family was surprised to hear the little child, rambling so patriotically about the ongoing issues in her nation. They couldn't freely look at their daughter. They wept, too.

"Honey, comfort your daughter," Leemu said to her husband, reaching out for a handkerchief to wipe Latto's face. "Everything will be okay. I know how you feel. I always feel that way, too."

While Dr. Kiamu was contemplating on what to say, there was an announcement for the passengers to board the plane. Pulling on one another to enter the plane, a gorgeous hostess welcomed each passenger and made sure that they were in the right plane.

As they were seated, Latto said, "Daddy, can you beg the hostess to stop the plane so that I can use the restroom?"

"Please honey, tell your Mom about that issue. That's a lady's problem." Dr. Kiamu was choking with laughter, but he couldn't allow it to explode for others to detect.

"How is it possible to stop a plane in the air for someone to attend a restroom?" Latto asked.

"Let's go to the back, there's a toilet facility within this plane," her mother said, passing ahead of her. "You know that your Daddy operates within his culture. He won't bring a female to a restroom."

Latto asked her father, when she returned to her seat from the restroom, "Do they have any other means to travel abroad besides planes?"

"Planes are the fastest means by which modern people like to travel. There are ships, trains, and vehicles. Do you want us to walk from Africa to cross the ocean by foot?" Dr. Kiamu joked. "That would take our lifetime, and the time of our unborn generations before we could ever reach America. In fact, many centuries ago many people were taken from Africa by ships across the Atlantic. They couldn't return to Africa because they had no access to ships. But today, we have numerous means and opportunities to travel. We can have our breakfast in Africa, lunch in Europe, and dinner in America on the same day."

Chapter 22

They were satisfied. The Kiamus had safely landed at their final destination, the modern land of milk and honey.

When Latto came out of the plane, still within the airport, she was very excited to see the beautiful horizon around her. She said, "This is the land I have dreamed about it. This is the land my people told me that one day I would dwell in. This is the land where all human beings are equal, important and recognized for what they do."

With joy, Latto prostrated and kissed the ground many times and said, "I see the reason my mother wanted me to survive. Who was there to have stopped her if she ever wanted to abort the pregnancy that brought me into this world? Who could have stopped my mother if she ever wanted to neglect me? But she endured every obstacle to make me the person the world will soon know her value of.

"No normal mother hates her child. No woman likes to see her children suffer. If it causes them to do anything, they would do it. They know that in the future their children would understand the reasons why their mothers did what was unreasonable to the world, but helped them survive."

Latto threw her eyes up in the air as if to say she could see her mother somewhere around her. She chanted in Kpelle "Thank you, my dear mother for all the care that you have given me. I will make you enjoy your last days on earth. When you have given up the ghost, I will bury you with our ancestors."

Some of the passengers and her parents stood in amazement, even though they couldn't understand all that Latto said in her dialect.

When Latto and her family came out of the airport, there was over twelve inches of snow, covering the land.

Latto said, "I see everybody dressed like a traditional dancer. I can't compare this place to any place I have seen. Besides my village, the Christian hospital, and Little France, I haven't seen any city like this. How do the people live in this city? How can I keep up with this kind of cold?"

Dr. Selma, a long time friend to the Kiamus, who once promised to help them in any way when they were still in Little France, had come to pick them up. She drove them to a local buffet restaurant for a dinner.

Latto saw everybody running to the food without someone serving them. She was baffled. She was terrified for her safety and that of her family. Trying to satisfy her curiosity, she asked her father, "How safe is this food?"

"Ninety-nine point nine, nine percent, honey," Dr. Kiamu answered Latto. "Why do you ask?"

"If the food is safe, will the owner make enough profit, when everybody is eating any amount?"

"For sure, Latto!"

"I can't believe it. I'm puzzled by the way everyone is playing in the food. I haven't seen that kind of marketing strategy before."

"First of all, the people that work here undergo periodic medical checkups in order to know that they are free from any communicable diseases," said Dr. Kiamu.

"The foods are also inspected periodically before the public consumption. There are a variety of ways they benefit. Some people eat more, while others eat less. People host different sorts of programs here. Some only order their food. If the proprietors weren't making enough profit, they would have closed the business. In fact, food is not a problem in the developed world, but the approach to understand some of the main causes and the management of people being overweight is one of their major problems."

Chapter 23

Before, Latto had lived in the world where they had been used to doing things manually. For instance, they washed their clothes with their hands. They spread them in the field or hung them on lines to dry and pressed them with coal irons. They walked many miles to buy their provisions. They had neither a school nor a hospital in their village. She had hated such a life, and she sought every opportunity to leave the village in order to experience the lives of others in other lands.

After a few days when Latto and her family went to do some laundry, she carefully watched her parents, load certain machines with their clothes, wash them, and then dry them, which seemed so amazing.

While going home, Latto saw her father put a plastic card into a machine and money began to pour out of it. Even at the filling station, her father swapped the same card in another machine and he began to pump gasoline into the rented vehicle by himself.

After watching all the fascinating things, Latto said, "I'm puzzled."

Her mother inquired, "Why are you surprised?"

"It appears the machines are doing everything for us," she said.

"You have a lot more to see, my child," her mother said as the family got in the car.

As her father drove them from the filling station, he said, "Let's go into the mall to buy some food for the house."

Latto looked at the others and then turned to her father and asked, "Daddy, can we stay home while you and Mommy go?"

"Why? Are you hungry?"

"Not exactly!"

"Why can't you go then?"

"I heard you talk about a morgue. I'm wondering what we are going to do in a dead people's place, when we are supposed to go to the store to buy the foodstuff. May be that was a slip of the tongue."

"I see your concern, Latto. You are used to the word, 'morgue,' meaning something else. The big stores in America are called malls. The place where they keep dead bodies before burial or identification is called a morgue or a mortuary as you have already said."

When they entered one of the malls, Latto watched her parents, collect the various items from every shelf. At the end, her mother used a self-service-payment counter. As her mother watched, she asked Latto, "I know you are ready to ask me again, because you do not understand why I am paying for the items through a machine when the workers are doing something else."

She asked, "Do you see those things hanging all around? Those are cameras. Besides recording every transaction and movement of all the people, they also are placed around for those who attempt to shoplift any item. In fact, most items have marks on them, which usually sound an alarm at the doorway to alert the management or the police that some wrong has been done."

Latto said, "Well, this nation belongs to educated people."

"That's why this government makes sure everybody reads and writes, unlike our nation, where a fewer number of people are educated and die from ignorance," her mother said.

During the next day, the Kiamu family went to the nearby school. The principal took them on a tour, showing them the facilities at the school. In the end, the Kiamus were convinced that the school was good.

Latto registered for the sixth grade according to her age level, while Manu and Numeh retained their respective grade levels.

When they went home, Dr. Kiamu hired a home-study teacher for his children, especially Latto who was placed in a higher class.

Within a short time, Latto adjusted. She made many friends and study mates.

Sometimes, some students irritated Latto by calling her all sorts of names, while others bullied her. Each time when her rights were infringed upon, she fought that person. Her parents were tired of receiving bad reports from the school about her.

They were concerned because they never wanted others to take them to be bad parents.

The morning after Latto fought some students on their way home from school, Dr. Kiamu called her, "We are thinking about sending you back to Africa, back to your village, Payeta. The day you are ready to stay with us, we will send for you."

Leemu quickly interrupted him by sending Latto back to her room. Then she said to her husband, "I don't think that's the right solution, Honey."

"Why do you stop me from saying what I want to say?"

"Because, I already know what you want to say," Leemu said. "You know that there's a war going on in Leewah. You have sacrificed to adopt Latto as your child. Any problem with a child needs to be addressed by the parents. So, you want to tell me that when Manu and Numeh misbehave, will you send them away? Will you send them to your parents when they are already in their graves? Who will train your children while you are still alive? Have you forgotten the meaning of adoption?

"Latto is now your legal child so as Manu and Numeh."

"Okay, what can we do?" he asked.

"Go to the principal and discuss how we both can deal with Latto."

"Do you think she will be interested in helping us again?" he asked. "Many times Latto has been punished, and she doesn't stop. The school is tired with her crazy behavior."

Her mother said, "I think the principal would feel happy to see the parents or guardians of a student who is creating problems come to discuss it. It is the job of the school to deal with students no matter what behavior they have. I know the principal will be happy to see me. In fact, the principal would like to see you as the father."

When the Kiamus got to school early one Monday morning, they were met by the principal, who seemed very happy to welcome them once again.

The principal said, "Well, Dr. Kiamu, children always need constant advice. I have children of my own. I know what it means to take care of them. "She had noticed the agony in his voice when he spoke about his daughter's behavior.

"One thing I have come to observe in my career and adult life is that children do not like aggression when it comes to educating or counseling them," she said. "Many children have been worse than Latto, and we have worked with them in school. They have turned out to be some of our most outstanding students. I can promise you that we are going to work with Latto. You will be surprised to see your child back where you want her to be."

"I hope so. I'm so disturbed. She wasn't like this when she was growing up," he said.

"Well, we shall place Latto in my special interest class," said the principal. "Once your cooperation as parents is exerted at the home level we will see what will be the outcome."

"I pledge to do my part! Thanks, Ma'am," Dr. Kiamu said as he walked with his wife out of the principal's office with a glimmer of hope.

Later, the principal led Latto into a quiet room and assured her, "Latto, feel free to tell me all that's been bothering you. You are part of my special interest group. I want you to be one of my best students. I know there is something that is bothering you and I'm sure you and I can find the solution."

Latto replied, "I become bothered and furious at the way some students put me down about my accent and color. They behave like animals, discriminating against me."

"You are absolutely right. I would feel the same way if I were in a community where people embarrassed me by calling me names or making fun about my accent or color. Know this Latto. Our accent as well as our color is one of the attributes God gives us," said the principal.

Latto, who hadn't looked in the principal's face, now, lifted her head up to listen to her with an encouraging smile, "You mean it?"

"Yes Latto, some people may use the sounds of an accent as a way of ridiculing others. Some may use it out of ignorance," the principal continued. "Every Language is difficult to speak. Its words have different meanings. Do you think we can work on this problem?"

"Yeah!"

"What do you think should we do first?"

"I want to know the correct meaning of the words like the other students," suggested Latto.

"You have given us the correct solution. We will do that. Hear this again, all travelers usually experience the same hurdles with communication. I experienced what you are going through when I came from Asia. No man sounds exactly like the other, even the same siblings. When I'm in a closed place, conversing with other people, any member of my family will recognize my voice."

Paving the way to make the depressed young lady comforted, the principal continued, "Latto, accent is one's own pattern of voice intonation that is delicate to that person. It can't easily be imitated by another person."

"Why then do most students behave like they did not understand me?"

"In the first place, most students always like to bully their peers who seem to be serious with their lessons. You would be surprised to know that most of the students who do not bully you are the studious ones.

"Furthermore, your accent is different from being unable to communicate fluently in any other language."

The principal clarified that when we are born in a certain environment and live there over a long time, we sound alike, which identifies us as people from that particular region. "No matter how long we stay in another nation, there will always be a trace of our original accent."

After the lengthy coaching, Latto told the principal, "Now I understand. I can assure you that I will not be bothered anymore when my peers call me names or talk about my accent." She went and hugged the principal.

The principal was happy to see Latto, smiling. She said, "Any problems please let me know."

In a few months, Latto once again became serious about her education. She was a member of the Language and Culture Diversity Club of the school. Her peers and the faculty members loved her. She had become fluent with the English language and her accent was understood, graduating with honors along with a scholarship to attend a university.

After spending four years at the university, Latto obtained a degree in counseling. Her parents were so thankful for her education.

Chapter 24

There had been great changes in Latto's life. Her physical appearance and mental capacity had developed immensely. She resembled her mother, Suah, with an average height and weight as a woman. Her dark skin emitted a natural beauty, while her tender eyes glowed within their sockets. Her broader hips were supported by her curved legs. Long hair had covered her one-time balding head. She appeared gorgeous in either her traditional attire or western dress.

A few years ago, if someone had ever told those who knew Latto how she would look, they couldn't have believed that person. No one can estimate the growth pattern of a girl child. After a few years, such a person would be surprised to see such a girl as his potential wife.

At twenty-three, having graduated from college, Latto parents' advice still jingled in her ears. She had the belief that only God could provide her a future husband.

Latto joined Manu who was still attending a university in a nearby city. She had not been happy, living without her sister. She wanted both of them to attend the same university. The differences in their career selections, led them to choose different universities.

Latto and Manu had gone to the McDonald's Restaurant one Friday for dinner. They saw a gentleman who allowed them to stand in front of him in the queue.

"Who's this young man?" Manu wondered, "It's uncommon for someone to give his or her space in a queue when everybody is rushing around at this time of the day."

They continued to look over their shoulders. Each time they did, their eyes landed in the eyes of the fellow.

"I wish this man knew that women are always bothered by the looks and thoughts of men having a crush on them," Latto said.

"I thought you are not watching him," Manu asked her sister.

They ordered their meals and sat in a corner, without taking any soft drink.

The fellow ordered his and then sat at the table ahead of them. As he continued to watch them, he asked, "Excuse me, ladies, which drink do you want?"

"Why do you want to be so nice to us?" Latto asked.

"As a gentleman seeing ladies, I must show some kindness. No one knows when and where we shall meet again."

"Okay! Sprite," said Manu.

"I need an orange," answered Latto.

He collected the drinks and carried them back to the ladies. He retired to his own table, avoiding further embarrassment for the ladies.

They continued to glance at the gentleman, smiling at one another.

"Don't let the young man know that we have a crush on him," Latto said. "I'm afraid that he will continue to hunt us like a bloodthirsty hunting dog. I don't want any of us to become his bait."

"That is true," Manu supported Latto. "You know men are quick to win the hearts of women, but the wise woman always knows how to play her cards."

Latto and Manu ate some of their food and threw the balance away. "Goodbye," said Manu to the gentleman.

"Please excuse me," the young man said. "Do you mind if I get your phone numbers?"

"Yes, I do," Latto stated, refusing to give it and leaving the place to go to her car.

"No problem," Manu said as she looked for something to write the number on. "Do you have a pad?"

"No, but write it in my palm," he said.

When Manu went to the car, Latto asked her. "Do you know the cost of what you have done? This guy will continue to hunt us like a shepherd dog."

"But he won't shoot me," Manu joked.

"Not you, but the booty," Latto said.

Both ladies laughed and quickly rushed home.

After they came home, Latto and Manu continued to talk about the kindness of the man. They wished every man in the city were like him.

"It seems like you are interested in this fellow," Latto said to her sister. "You are condemning other men yet gratifying a man who behaves like any other men.

"Every man behaves the same way when they are blinded by love," she continued. "When they see women for the first time, they want to do extra things to make a good impression. But when they have acquired what they want out of a woman, they put on the coat of their real selves."

"It's true. But we can't extend that generalization to every man," said Manu. "Even the few bad men among them taint the names of all men."

A few months had passed and during one afternoon, Manu's phone rang with a set of strange numbers. She hesitated to answer the call. Latto encouraged her to respond. It was a call from Kenda, the gentleman whom they had met at the McDonald's Restaurant a few weeks ago.

"Hi Kenda! We hope everything is okay with you? asked Manu.

"I'm alright," he said.

"That's cool. Hey Kenda, we are wondering…uh—uh. I wonder if you would take time one day…to visit us. If you aren't able to, forget it. One day, we will meet and have some time for a discussion," Manu hesitated as she uttered her selected words slowly to avoid gales of laughter.

"What about tomorrow afternoon? Can we meet at the Applebee's Restaurant right down the hill around at two P.M.?"

"No problem! Thank you," Manu replied with an excitement. She quickly turned and looked at her sister. They both laughed and hugged one another.

"It seems like you are deep into this guy's life." said Latto.

"What do you want me to do?" asked Manu.

"Well, I would be happy to have a brother-in-law."

"You are not serious," Manu said.

As they selected their dresses for church and for their meeting at Applebee's Restaurant, Manu asked her sister, "Latto, how do you like this green dress?"

"Why can't you wear the striped gray and black dress?"

"Well, it makes me look kind of fat in my stomach," Manu complained.

"Okay, the green isn't a bad color for women," said Latto.

"What are you wearing?" Manu asked as she walked toward their closet.

"I will wear the dress Daddy bought for me. I would like to wear it because I'm missing Daddy," Latto said.

In the afternoon, the ladies were the first to appear at the Applebee's Restaurant.

As they sat for some time, Manu asked her sister, "Do you think this gentleman will show up?"

"Oh, Manu! Don't worry; I think he's just running late. Guys are never on time except on their wedding day," Latto joked.

While they were still pondering what to do, Kenda appeared.

"There he comes, speaking of the Devil," Latto joked.

"My dear ladies, please pardon me. I don't want to take your precious time to explain my problems. I'm only sorry for keeping you for so long. I hope you haven't" been here the whole day?" he asked as he showed remorse.

"Not too long," Manu answered.

"May I get you guys something to drink?" a young lady came to the table and began to write their orders.

As they were eating, Kenda opened up the conversation, "Ladies, what do you do during the day…go to school, work or something?"

"I graduated from college just a few months ago. I'm working in a jewelry manufacturing center as the assistant supervisor," Latto responded.

"Beautiful," Kenda nodded.

"What about you, Manu?"

"I'm a graduating senior at the public university downtown. I also work at a drug treatment center," Manu answered.

"Well, that's good. You have a bright future."

"What about you?" Manu asked.

"Well, I hold a master's degree in anthropology. I produce documentaries mainly on Africa. Originally, my parents migrated from Africa when I was three years old. My entire life has been spent in this nation. I wish to travel to Africa one day. Our kinsmen are still alive. My mother usually visits them.

Chapter 25

Kenda was a promising young man in his late twenties. He had been rehearsing how to approach Latto about his affection for her. He had been looking for a moral-minded lady like Latto to declare his intention to her for a lasting companionship. He did not want to rush into it and ruin the opportunity. He spent several months, taking Latto to dinner or to some important places without Manu.

Surprisingly, Manu had been moody about the affair. She felt that her sister had used her with Kenda. She thought Latto knew that she had a crush on Kenda from the first day they met him at the McDonald's Restaurant.

Recalling the harmonious events of their past, Manu said, "I will not allow bad blood to get into our family business. She's my sister. I will let her go ahead with Kenda. I may let her know my feeling one day when Kenda isn't around. Perhaps, I should just forget about it to become a good sister-in-law."

With all their outings, Latto and Kenda had been very careful, respecting one another's boundaries as they remained morally chaste.

One afternoon at the National Aquarium, seeing the marine creature, swimming around them, Kenda finally gained the courage. He took the bold step and asked Latto, "Please pardon me. I don't want to embarrass you."

"Oh no, feel free! So long as you respect the boundaries of women, I have no problem."

Then, Kenda asked her, "Do you have any idea about the kind of man you would like to have as your future husband?"

"Why are you asking me?"

"I just want to know what you think about guys." Kenda replied.

"Do you want to plan my life now?"

"Uh, not exactly."

"But partially, right?"

"Maybe, something like that."

"Let me ask you, my friend. Why men are so quick to be concerned about women? When a woman comes a bit closer to them, they always want to open up their entire body to embrace her."

"You know, that's what we are. Generally men are always interested in coming around good women for satisfaction. Once we are accepted in the presence of good women, we feel that we are on top of the entire world. That is why we do some stupid things before we get to know that they were not the right things."

"Oh yeah! Do you think I'm one of your good women?"

"Yes. Don't you think so? Do you think if you were one of them, I could have come around you?"

"Maybe."

"No young man wants to come around the unattractive or less cared ladies."

"How do you know?" Latto said. "You haven't been seeing me that long. You don't know how I control my anger or my temperament when I'm confronted with difficult situations."

"How long does it take to know a zebra from baboon? You are one of the good people," Kenda said as he affectionately smiled and looked straight into her eyes.

Latto bowed her head. She smiled, trying to control her shyness.

She began, "You know, Kenda, I have two set of parents—my biological and my adoptive parents—they both have been married for all these years. They hate the humiliating stories surrounding a divorce. My adoptive parents are well educated, and they are devout Christians. They want to be proud of us, by having us marry and staying with our husbands for life.

"This is why I have devoted all my life in school and in the church, because I want moral wisdom and spiritual knowledge."

Kenda said, "Your parents aren't alone. Parents want to hear good things about their children."\

"Okay, let me tell you my mindset. It may be the absolute truth for other women. It may seem archaic. It's the saying of every moral-minded woman. Don't think I'm the first to say it," she said.

"Oh no, go ahead. I have no problem. I'm the patient dove," Kenda said.

She said, "I plan to marry a guy that respects the value of humanity. He must be an enduring person no matter the test of circumstances around him. You know God made each person as a one of kind. Nobody can be like another person in personality, love and strength. So my husband must understand my biological makeup and try to live by it."

"That's the mistake we always make. We want to be like other people. It's a difficult job to copy another person," said Kenda.

"Sometimes, you try to have the same mind as others, but their minds are always different from yours. I'm praying that the young man I marry should be concerned with my morality rather than my physique. I don't want him to compare me to other women."

"I knew you could say that. Women are mindful about how men care for them," Kenda said as he gazed at Latto with an adoring look.

"Since you asked me, please let me make myself perfectly clear," Latto said.

"I'm sorry for the interruption. Please, go ahead."

"As human beings, women aren't always right. When I'm wrong about a certain issue, my husband should have the courage to correct me without, allowing emotions to play into it. I believe that the best place for any rebuke between married couple is in a private place, which is their bedroom. When it's done there, no past issue should be carried over into future talks. If it is brought up again, it would resurrect the already settled problem.

"Women like men who approach issues with tenderness. Condemnation is our enemy. You know what I mean, right?"

"Absolutely," Kenda replied. "Every woman needs a bold man - a man who is a good communicator and a man who encourages his wife and children. How can you spend your days with a man who does not provide freedom and love?"

"Say that again, my lad. How can I spend my days with a predator?

"I want to have a happy family, Kenda, rather than to be embarrassed with my husband's bizarre lifestyle."

"So true," Kenda quickly said, trying not to interrupt Latto.

"A man who won't sleep until his pet is afforded a loaf of bread is a good husband. Men like to brag about their wealth, their wives, their children, their jobs, even their education. I don't want my husband to be that wasteful. I'm not saying that my husband shouldn't spend, but he must account for any amount of money he spends on a justifiable purpose. Do you know what I mean?"

"Yes, go ahead. You are on course," Kenda encouraged.

"The Lord will determine the number of children we intend to have. We shall take every preventive measure about our health not to neglect the children, without using the words "unwanted children" against any of them. My biological mother warned my adoptive parents about me before I was adopted. My husband should be a law-abiding citizen, a man who will always ask God to do the right thing; even when no one else is doing it."

As Latto straightened her dress, she said, "I need a man who isn't abjectly poor or extremely rich, but educated with an excellent bill of health. What about that? Look, I don't want a wife-murderer. Do you understand that?"

"Latto, I'm overwhelmed with your brilliant dialogue. I didn't know you could talk like this. You have always been quiet whenever I have interacted with you and Manu."

Trying to select his words wisely, Kenda said, "I grew up with many girls. My Grandmother, Garmah, raised me. I'm used to being around women. I love women. I hate to see their rights being infringed."

He continued, "I'm praying to my Lord to find the right woman, a virtuous woman as a wife. I wish you to be that person. I would be that happiest person on earth. When we get married, I pray that we endure every life situation. I don't want to marry a second time."

"Well, Kenda, you are showing me that you think you are the man."

"What do you think?"

"If I were a professor, I would give you an A."

"Really?"

"Yes, you deserve it, but since you belong to the masculine group, I can't give too many praises to you too soon. My mother used to say that all men are like a python that doesn't care for all the other body segments, except the tail. When you step on it, it's ready to spring on to you. Most men always pretend to be good. When they get what they want, they change in to their actual character." She looked at Kenda and smiled.

"I know, I know," Kenda interrupted. "I know I don't want to go that route. I'm not in any hurry. I'm dedicated to you and only you at the moment."

"Hey, may I ask you for something?"

"Oh yes! Go ahead, no problem."

"Am I the model woman an African man or any other man would need, especially to be his wife?"

"What do you mean, my dear? You are gorgeous who else could you be…"

"You know…you know, don't pretend! You don't mean what you are saying."

"For real, I don't know. What are you talking about?"

"Well, let it stay like that; next time I will tell you since you don't know your taste for women as an African."

"Come on…Are you talking about the sizes of women? You don't know that most African men like big sized women?" he asked. "There is an adage that says, 'when a man marries a big sized woman, he would be respected that he is taking a good care of her.'"

"Huh, What would you say about western men, too?"

"It's the other way around. Most of them like small sized ladies."

"That isn't true."

"Well, if that's a myth, okay? My thinking is different."

"But look, let me tell you. I know the importance of life. I can't starve myself just to be the size a man would want me to be. I don't want to kill myself with a certain disease, because I don't want to eat enough to gain extra weight."

"Look Latto! I'm myself. I can't be like the other men. I was raised under a strict custom. I'm a man from a little town. I relate to the life of my old folks, rather than those in our real world. Once I have found the lady of my choice, why can't I be grateful to render her my unfailing love? I hope she will be in a position to love me, too."

Latto nodded as she continued to look at Kenda with a big smile.

He admonished her as he carried his mouth closer to her right ear and whispered, "I need a strong, independent, and loving woman, whether African, eastern, western…you name the rest. The most important thing is to have good health and love from the bottom of the heart. I don't care whether a woman is big or slim. I'm not after the size of the woman. I'm after a moral one."

Chapter 26

The day was Friday when Latto and Kenda met at the Kiamus' house in the afternoon. It was the moment every young woman wished for. They want someone to tell them the truth, not to flatter them about a lasting relationship.

Like most young men usually do when they are in the mood of approaching ladies, Kenda bowed his head and smiled to drive away the anxiety. He said, "I want to surprise you today, Latto."

Latto looked at him with curiosity as she listened.

Then the young suitor lifted up his head, looking in Latto's eyes and continued. "I can't pick up the words to tell you what I have wanted to tell you."

Before Latto could ask Kenda about what he was trying to say, several groups of people gathered at the family house. They were singing and dancing, throwing grains of rice everywhere as their West African tradition demands it.

Suddenly, Mosiah appeared among the group and gladly said, "May the Lord of our ancestors and heaven watch this place. May he provide us all the blessings we need. Anybody whose mind will perceive any evil among us, may he be dragged to the kingdom of hell."

All the people present answered together.

"Our doctor, our nurse and other relatives of Latto, we believe that when we find what we like, we must go for it. We have come to harvest vegetables in your backyard. We want to plant some in our yard," Mosiah said.

"Do we have any vegetable planted?" Dr. Kiamu asked as he lay against the sofa.

"I'm referring to your daughter, Latto. We have come to betroth her as the expectant wife for my nephew Kenda," Mosiah explained. "I'm presenting these sets of African suits, one to the father of the bride, and the other to the mother."

According to the African culture, Mosiah gave a set of rings to his nephew, Kenda and cautioned him to find his heart among some girls who were seated amongst the people. Kenda walked among the people and went to Latto and bowed.

"Here's the symbol of my love for you. I want you as my future wife." He grabbed one of her fingers and placed the ring on it. Then the group applauded.

Latto sniggered as a lucky woman. She looked at her father, then went and collapsed into his arms. They both wept with joy. Then her father patted her on the back and said, "That's fine. Do what is right, Babygirl. Do you love him?"

"I love him. But please talk to his people for me."

"I always do the best things for my children. All parents are always concerned about their children, especially the girls," said Dr. Kiamu. "I don't want Latto to be exposed to marriage, when the man isn't ready to keep a wife. My wife and I have no objection against your proposal. Since this is an engagement, we will see how things unfold. My blessing goes with them as they strive to be successful."

A few months later, the right time finally came. Everyone had been preparing for Latto's wedding. She and Manu were so excited about it. They had been talking and planning it during the course of six months.

At least one of them was on the way to meet the expectation of their parents and other relatives. Even though marriage was the right thing for young people, it's advisable to be prepared before engaging into it.

Dr. Kiamu and his wife had dreamed about their children, obtaining college or graduate degrees before settling with their respective families. They couldn't stop the engaged couple now in any way, so like any good parents they must allow God into do whatever would happen.

Latto's parents were impressed that one of their daughters was making them proud.

Her mother said, "The wise child who washes his hands usually dines with kings, queens, princes or princesses. I believe that Latto is a trained child and does things right. I pray for a bright future for their marriage."

In a moment the hall was quiet and everything was set for the wedding.

Dr. Selma, who was sitting with the Kiamu family, said to Dr. Kiamu, "This is your day. You know I have passed through this road two times now. It is a good thing to remain alive, while your children are wedded."

While officiating at the ceremony the minister said, "I believe you both have done your homework and are satisfied with one another. Marriage isn't a strange institution. No matter what condition comes into the marriage, whether good or bad, it's the responsibility of the couple to work out things to survive it.

"The day any of you considers a divorce as an option to separate your union, let that person call all the people present today to be present during the time of the divorce before it can be granted," the minister warned. "In the sight of God, there's no graduation from the institution of marriage. It would be better for a man or a woman not to engage into any marriage than to break up."

"You the family members, friends, and loved ones should always be in the position to give them some pieces of constructive advice to sustain their marriage. I warn that none of us should blame them if they begin to drive us away from their business due to our unwelcome comments and actions against their will," the minister concluded.

A day after the wedding the newly married couple went to Sin City for a one-week honeymoon. The weather was extremely hot.

The most amazing thing was that when they entered the city at night, they thought it was daytime from the magnificent light that illuminated it.

Most of their outings were done during the night since the weather was a little bit cooler than during the day. They planned how they could spend the rest of their lives on earth during this time. They planned the number of children they wanted. They agreed on family finances: budgeting and banking their income together.

"What does it mean for us to save our income separately? I don't think it was wise for us to marry, if we plan to have separate accounts," Latto said.

"I'm not good at saving, so I entrust you with the responsibility over our finances," Kenda said.

"I think I'm vulnerable to restricting children," said Latto. "I will look up to you to make sure that our children receive the best counsel."

They both considered the need to help less fortunate people in society. Since they had the same African background, they planned to undertake some developmental projects there.

As he was always surprising his wife, Kenda once again said, "Latto, I had planned to tell you something as a surprise after our marriage. Today is the right time to tell you."

"What must that be? It couldn't be my death warrant." Latto jokingly interrupted, praying that she shouldn't receive any negative news that would derail their marriage.

"No, don't be frightened," Kenda, said. "My grandfather Kuaka was a world-class businessman. He owned business firms around the world. He had one son, Zuedai, my father.

Zuedai died from a fatal car accident before his father. Being that I'm the nearest heir, my grandfather, Kuaka, passed every piece of his legacy over to me."

Latto laid her left hand on Kenda's right shoulder and said, "Tell me something. Why didn't you tell me already? I thought men didn't have the stomach to keep secrets from women."

"Not this man," Kenda replied. "The last thing for a man to do is to reveal all his secrets to a woman who isn't yet his wife. All men should learn from Samson and Delilah. Men who don't live by the rules always lose their lives."

"Well, not all women wish to kill their husbands. I know it isn't what you want to hear," Latto smile. "You are a nice man any woman would wish to spend her life with."

"Thank you," Kenda said as he informed Latto, "Let me tell you that I'm so proud of you. I'm sure I didn't make any mistake in having you all to myself."

Then Latto glanced at Kendal and smiled. When she thought of how her mother, Suah had struggled with her marriage, her children, her daily needs, and her family. She appreciated Kenda.

"So, before his death, Kuaka directed me to engage in humanitarian works," Kenda revealed. "I have been waiting to get married before undertaking my dreams."

"No problem, Kenda. I can assure you that our nation, my village, will be the first place for us to undertake some projects," Latto suggested. Latto couldn't believe that she had married a millionaire. She imagined the dream of her mother when she said, "Latto, I'm not only thinking about buying a doll baby for you after we have sold our charcoal. I didn't have the opportunity to attend any formal school so that I could read and write my name. My mind has remained dark to the white man's civilization. I don't regret my life; it is such a life that made me who I'm today, but I want yours to be better."

Latto imagined her mother telling her, "Your hair will cover your balding head. People like Wianneh and Zonpu, won't laugh at you. You will find a loving young man to marry you. You both will ride the jet plane and live together in the land of opportunities. You will be our primary source our knight in shining armor to develop our village and its environs."

Chapter 27

Almost three years after Latto's wedding, Vidia, her childhood friend, came to visit her. Vidia had been overwhelmed with insecurity in her marriage with Kwemeh, which stopped her from visiting as frequent as her friends wanted her to do.

Latto was bringing in some things when Vidia suddenly slammed the front door of her car on her son's fingers. She shouted, "I have killed my baby, I've killed my baby…" She then dropped her suitcase and picked up the crying child. She ran in the direction where Latto stood.

Latto quickly grabbed the child and put the wounded fingers in her mouth to blow on them. She said, "You will be fine, honey. I am sorry; your mommy did not mean to mash your fingers."

Vidia was confused, crying and hitting things here and there. In her agony, she displayed her marital predicament at her child, since her husband was not around. "This boy is very troublesome like his father. I have come to spend a little time with my friend and then he wants to cause problems for me."

"Vidia, the child is not at fault. It is needless to talk about that now. Let us go to the clinic next door. Let the doctors see his fingers. Something serious may be wrong," Latto encouraged her friend.

Latto's friend had always run from her home each time she and her husband had a marital fuss.

Vidia and her husband came from two different countries. They were the first people from their respective families to travel outside of their motherlands. They had the responsibility to support their respective families every month. They were also responsible to pay their bills here as well.

Vidia and Kwemeh had kept a separate account, handling their financial affairs without consulting one another. Kwemeh was unable to pay all the bills since support was not coming from vidia. The companies had threatened them to disconnect the phone and electricity services.

Vidia seemed depressed. Even her appearance alone could tell anybody who had known her before that she wasn't handling things very well in her marriage. She thought leaving her home for a while could bring her some sort of joy.

Latto knew that these problems always occur in all married homes. Nobody should be quick to approach them. Nobody likes trouble, especially troubles in the married home. Grown-up people should always discuss their disagreement to find a common understanding.

Latto told Vidia, "I've heard all you have said, but let us find some food for the children. In the evening when my husband comes home, we will decide what to do next."

Suddenly, there was a knock at the front door." Latto rushed to the door. It was her husband, Kenda. The six-foot tall man hugged and kissed Latto at the doorway, while she held his bag in one hand.

"Wahoo, am I seeing things? May be I need some eyeglasses. Is that Vidia! How are you?"

"Well, I am the person I think you know, Kenda."

"How are things with you?"

"I am just hanging in there because I have to."

"Come on Vidia; say something better than that, girl! You have not quit with all your smart sayings."

Vidia looked at Latto, and they both laughed, and she hugged Kenda. Kenda hugged her again, and said, "Welcome, my girl. You look good. Kwemeh got some nice woman."

"Yes, uh…! Nice woman, who he does not talk nice about."

"Okay, I know you women do not always appreciate our effort. How are little Koido and his father?"

"Kwemeh is fine, but Koido is in the room sleeping." Vidia hesitated to let Kenda know that she had smashed his fingers.

When Kenda went to his room to change his clothes, his boys followed and informed him that Vidia had smashed her child's fingers.

Kenda went into the kitchen and asked, "Vidia, what has happened to little Koido?"

Vidia said, "We wanted you to eat and rest before telling you, since it wasn't serious. Anyway, I slammed the car's door on my baby's fingers today. We carried him to doctors and he is fine."

They laughed as they set the table for supper. "I told you, men were born with children in their stomachs. My husband is ready to fight us for the child. He will not understand, he will continue to find out why such a thing should happen to Koido," said Latto as she whispered to her friend.

The following day, Kwemeh went to Latto and Kenda to find out about his wife. He was delighted when he finally met Vidia and their son there. He had earlier thought about informing the police about his wife's disappearance. Consulting some security personnel, he was advised to search all possible and usual areas before reporting anything to the police.

After they had completed some of the evening activities, Kenda and Latto called Vidia and Kwemeh. They informed Kwemeh the purpose for which his wife came to them. Latto advised them to highlight the root-cause of their problems.

Vidia began, "Latto and Kenda out of respect for you, I am going to let you know some of the attitudes of Kwemeh. If I say I will explain all that he has been doing to me, we will get nothing today."

"Please say all what you know is bothering you and we will listen. All that we are after is to see you and Kwemeh once again strong in your family life. You know that it is not good to hold back bad feelings. Anger tends to be the oasis for stress and untimely death." Kenda smiled as he encouraged Vidia.

"Kwemeh has destroyed the love that I had for him. He seems so crazy with destructive jealousy until he doesn't even know whom he actually wants to accuse me of being in love with. He does not allow me to own a cell phone. When he comes home, he will check the caller-ID to identify the strange numbers and names he may have seen. When we go out, he does not want me to talk with anybody. He always questions my movement with friends at work or in the community. Friends have stopped communicating with me. I am isolated, Latto. How can I live without friends or people to communicate with?

"Kwemeh seems very angry sometimes whenever he hears something about me. He sometimes leaves our apartment and sleeps away for many days. For months he won't eat with me and won't talk about any plan or discuss anything with me. He knows very well that since I was a young lady, he has been the only man I have shared my love with. Maybe he feels because I am innocent to many things, I am stupid.

"Look, Latto my life is miserable and I do not want to continue living that way with Kwemeh. I think he is pushing me closer to the idea of a divorce, I think that will be the last episode of our marriage. Let him be free to do whatever he has been denied from doing."

Vidia wept. She regretted that she did not take into consideration all the pieces of advice her parents gave her concerning a hasty marriage. She had gone to England to visit her aunt when she met Kwemeh and got pregnant. They married a month later. She came to the United States with her newly wedded husband. A few months later, she agreed to the fact that she was blind with the infatuated love. She had her dearly beloved man who had turned out to be unloving.

"Kwemeh, have you heard your wife? It seemed like there is a little problem in your home. As I said earlier, please tell us what we can do to make your home become a little heaven once again," Kenda said.

"Yes, it is true. You know I do not like to talk much. I always like to deal with people, especially women fairly. Vidia and I do not have complicated problems. Most of them are simple. Since I felt that they were insignificant, I continued to overlook them until they overtook our marriage. I am sorry it has come to this. However, whatever our problems maybe, I can't dispute the fact that Vidia is a caring, loving and hardworking woman. I beg her to continue holding on to those values she possesses.

"Some of our misunderstandings, if not the major one, has centered on money. We do not budget our finances together. We do not have one account. We do not budget how to pay our various bills. I do not know what she does with her money from the two jobs she had been doing. In fact, she has got herself entangled with credit card debts. When we got married I told her the good and the bad things about credit cards. She ignored the advice. Any credit card that came to her, she used it. Now, her credit is ruined. It is affecting her auto insurance. She knew very well that nothing is done in the developed world without having good credit. I thought she would have listened to me to maintain her credit.

"Despite all of that, I pay all the bills, including her car notes. We have two cars. I advised Vidia that we should not buy another car on credit since we have two cars already paid for. She refused and took out another expensive loan on a car.

"She sends money home without discussing it with me first. Several times when I attempted to advise her, she would call the police and make statements about what I said out of context."

Kwemeh continued, "There are many private issues that, I think are unhealthy for me to continue explaining about when they will not benefit any. What I think will benefit our family is peace. I believe I married someone that I could live in harmony with, to not be fussing every day with. Why must I be coming in my own home and be afraid of my own wife? When the world has raised my temper, my wife should be there to calm it.

"Once again, I want you to please talk to Vidia into coming home. I need her at home. I do not want our children to suffer or hate us in the future for our thoughtlessness. I will try this time to go along with what she wants our marriage to be. "

"Vidia, you have heard your husband and you can see what he is doing before you. He is performing what our culture does by squatting and holding your legs, begging you to forget everything and be the wife you are. It is not an easy thing for two people who were trained in different homes, with different attitudes to decide to uphold their marital vows. No counselor will enter the married couple's hearts to know the things that are happening in their lives. The couple may feel embarrassed to explain their actual problems. I believe every man wants to maintain his privacy. You are your own counselor, if you agree to let the bad blood to go away in your marriage," Kenda said. "Every marriage has problems, but the management of the problems is love. Love does not come from one person. Love is a give and take from both parties. If a person does not give in at times, it will always be difficult to find love. As human beings, we sacrifice at times before we can get what we want."

Latto also emphasized, "I heard you talk about a divorce. Do not let that cross your mind. If a person wants to avoid something that is dreadful and humiliating, he should first avoid the thought about getting a divorce. No person wants to experience the dilemma of a divorce. It is the worse behavior ever invented by men and women. The worse thing about a divorce is that all parties are victims: the woman, the man, the children as well as all relatives and friends, even people just hearing about it will sometimes feel embarrassed and remorseful. A divorce only benefits the devil."

Latto concluded, "We are hoping that you, especially Vidia, will put all these things behind you and begin to work with your husband. I know you want to build a future for your children. My friend always says, 'If you fail to do well for yourself and your family, nobody would do it better.' So, Vidia, times are passing by us gradually as we get older and older everyday. This is the time to plan to establish our mutual families."

After Latto and Kenda had advised them, the disputed couple finally hugged one another and rendered apologies for all they had done to each other. They also thanked Latto and her husband for being there to settle their marital conflict. They became embarrassed and sorry for what they had done by washing their "dirty linens" before other people.

Chapter 28

After years, Latto finally returned to her birth-land, Leewah. Her return was celebrated like that of a rock star coming to entertain her fans. The ten huts in Payeta had been colorfully decorated. The grasses had been neatly cut. Palm branches were hanging everywhere.

As Latto aroused the emotions of the crowd by dancing with them, Chief Jao hobbled, took a feeble glance as old age was weighing him down.

Dokpa Jao was the chief of Payeta when the Kiamus adopted Latto. Coming back, while he was still alive was a tremendous blessing for him and the villagers.

Latto humbly knelt before the chief and introduced her husband, Kenda, and her engineer, Yomee. "We have come with many projects for our area," she said.

The crowd interrupted her with applause. The chief limbed toward Latto and her team. He shook their hands. The crowd once again quieted to listen.

Latto revealed, "My organization, Latto's Humanitarian Organization along with help from other humanitarian people around the world, will connect Payeta to the main road with a modern forty-five mile paved road. Schools are going to be built not only in Payeta but also in the villages around here. A hospital with a refuge center for the destitute will also be built. Scholarships are available for young people in this region and the surrounding area.

"We must also thank the people who provided the funds for these projects. It is also our responsibility to see that the projects are carried out as planned."

Chief Jao marveled, "I don't think this is true. It is too good to be our true. I can't imagine us entering into the long-awaited modern civilization. I can't imagine that I have stayed alive to see our village developed."

"Such wonderful news and the return of our daughter can't go on without performing our traditional ritual to grace the sacredness from our God." Chief Jao commanded every hut head to bring a white rooster for the sacrifice.

As the various sacrificial items were produced, the chief zoë of the village led the ceremony. Everyone was present, even representatives from the surrounding villages. All participated in the ritual as a surety that no one among them had an evil-mind against the projects.

The one-year project turned the village into a mini-city. Latto encouraged investors to invest in Leewah. Jobs were available for most people, and they supported the initiatives of the central government.

Seeing herself at the zenith of this opportunity, Latto marveled that her dream, even the blessings of her mothers, had come to light. "The pieces of advice from mothers are always the soils of nurture for their children no matter how long it takes, success is always achieved at the end of the tunnel," she said.

When she looked back at her life, Latto imagined the many good choices she had made through good people. She praised all, including her mothers for the mountains they climbed, the valleys they went into their hollows, and the rivers they swam during difficult days in search for a better life.

No one believed that such a transformation could have ever been achieved due to the indolent life of most of her family members. For instance, Yallon was known as the cane-juice sucker, the corpus smoker or the producer of the cussing bomb in the village. Everyone made a mockery of him as a lazy man. Her uncle Torkolon had lived the unacceptable life, more than any of his colleagues.

She imagined herself as a girl from a ten-hut village, from a poverty-stricken family who only spoke Kpelle. She recalled the time she had never lived anywhere, and had no connection to any profiled name; no family member had a plantation or bank account. She imagined the time no one was a product of western civilization, if any of them saw their name written as big as an elephant, they would not recognize it.

Even though most of her relatives died during the civil war, Latto was thankful to see a few of them still around. Wianneh, who once called her a hairless skull, had made several trips abroad as well as Zonpu and Jucuma. Yallon spent some time in jail and worked on the government farm for drinking a bitter root with liquors. Nuwoe had obtained a certain medicine from Gayflor, the top herbalist, to stop his brother from drinking and smoking addiction. Once again Yallon and Suah became close and enjoyed the fruits of Latto.

Chapter 29

"I can't believe it! Who is this Latto?" Rev. Kelikow said. As the newly ordained minister of one of the most renowned parishes in town, he was trying to control his anxiety when he dropped a piece of oily roasted cassava on the only prepared copy of his speech. He said, "I don't think she's the Latto, my cousin, I knew in Leewah."

Rev. Kelikow went closer to the television set, wishing to take in a deeper glimpse at the fading advertisement clip about an upcoming project to be undertaken by Latto's Humanitarian Organization in Leewah. Even the sentences at the bottom of the screen could not bring forth the information he needed. He then turned on his lap-top and googled Latto and Latto's Humanitarian Organization. From the little description he read, he was convinced that she was the Latto from Payeta. He continued to contemplate as he talked to himself, wiping the spilled oil from his paper.

He rushed to the phone on the table. Several times, he dialed the number he copied from the advertisement. An answering machine always responded and asked him to leave his name, phone number, and a message.

As Rev. Kelikow lay in the cushion by the table anxiously, waiting for a response from the messages he left for Latto. It appeared like he had gone into a trance. He entered a certain room along with Latto. But the room appeared dark. There were many people, jubilating for the purpose which neither Rev. Kelikow nor Latto understood. Emerging from their rears came countless numbers of dreadful animals, each with one leg, one eye, one hand, and one nostril respectively. They began to strike the people with all forms of calamities. Rev Kelikow saw them survive in tears and resentments. For him, he felt the one that had already planted its roots within his bloodstream. He was forced to endure the agonizing treatment. At the end, the calamities were revealed to him as an affliction previous generations in Leewah had already encountered. He considered the calamities as the many wars brought by real people to whom the people of Leewah were less than equipped to challenge. The calamities also reminded him to believe that any achievement during their suffering was less than what they lost or what they should have obtained during their normal state of mind. He said that besides their lives, the difference was their blessing, national legacy, pride, and self-esteem robbed by the powerful hands they had known very well.

Suddenly, Rev. Kelikow woke up and began to contemplate on the meaning of the dream. Then, he received a knock at his door, informing him about Latto, his hometown girl, living next door in Christopolis. (This city, where she lived, named after a biblical Christ, was the capital of Leewah, which represented the rushing place where people from all walks of life strived for the golden answers to their anticipated desires).

As he was summoned, he entered a magnificent building, and he stepped on the colorful carpets. There, he met Latto surrounded by a garrison of dedicated friends and relatives like the royal queen in her villa.

When Latto spotted the short nice looking man coming through the front door, she rushed on him and threw herself on the man, assuming that he was Rev.Kelikow.

"I don't think I'm making any mistake," said Latto. "I don't think I can easily miss my own brood. Am I seeing the Kelikow I knew?"

"Yes, it is he."

"See how bright and nice looking my man is. He has not changed at all."

"For real! People always flatter me that I'm the replica of Neh Korto, our maternal grandmother," Rev. Kelikow responded. "There is nothing good in this skin besides long life."

"So true," Latto answered.

A chain of introductions seemed unnecessary between Latto and Rev. Kelikow. Just by the first glimpse, it was enough for both of them. From the noticeable birthmark on Latto's right face and a surgical scare of a little growth on her left foot, Rev. Kelikow also realized that she was his father's sister's daughter whom he left in their village, Payeta. She seemed to be no different from Suah)with an attractive physical makeup and a humorous appearance.

Rev. Kelikow wondered how such a dramatic change could have occurred within a short period. Before going abroad for further studies, Rev. Kelikow had gone to Payeta to get some parental blessings from Neh Korto, his paternal grandmother. By the time he left the little girl, Latto in the village, he didn't have the least idea that she would have become a westernized woman. After all, he became impressed about her development, and that another educated person had been added to their small family.

"I'm happy to see you again Rev. Kelikow. Welcome, come and have a seat right by me." She held him by the right hand as they went to a cushion chair in the living room, facing the portrait of the giant female chimpanzee with her three young chimps hanging on the wall.

Rev Kelikow relaxed beside her and appeared calm with his eyes wide-open to see the fascinating things around him and missing the least detail that his missionary trip to Christopolis could turn out to be a family's affair. It turned out to be the biggest surprise of his life, and how long his trip and visit could last were uncertain.

Latto came, sat beside Rev. Kelikow and asked him for the whereabouts of each and every member of the family she thought he might know. It was her way of detecting how close their relationship was blended. She fed him with soft drinks and fried vegetable rice, deliciously prepared as a taste from the Leewah nation.

"I know you still like our native food?" Latto asked Rev. Kelikow.

"Yes, as a matter of fact, a few hours ago I couldn't pass by some women I saw at the hotel grounds, selling some roasted cassava and fish with some hot pepper sauce like the ones we used to eat many years ago when I was here," Rev. Kelikow said. "I remembered how grandma and other women used to fix the cassava in many forms: the dump-ball, the farina, and the fufu for our dinner. I was eating the one I bought when I read your advertisement about the work you are doing among our people."

"I can fix you a better one. Rev. Kelikow, just inform me about what else you need. I want you to feel at home," Latto would say. "Do you know what it means to come across your own blood? Do you?"

"I do!" Rev. Kelikow responded with an unexpected joy pervading his inner being, which he couldn't resist.

"Never did I think that I could come across you in this wide world again," Latto said. "Do you remember when I was eight years old and you left for studies?"

"I do."

"Do you see that I'm a grown up woman with three children? That means I'm no longer the child you left a couple years ago," Latto said. "This house is the second one in this town, besides the couple I own elsewhere."

"Thank you, cousin," Rev. Kelikow said. "I have also borne four beautiful children, one boy and three girls."

"I have continued to think about you, but I couldn't figure out your whereabouts. I have only concluded that your well-being had become another unfortunate story like our family did when they experienced the hurt about Uncle Jimmy, your kidnapped father," she said.

Rev. Kelikow answered her, "I made it as my goal to chase the smallest particle of opportunity all the days I was abroad, and such a life has made me who I'm today. The decade of civil war kept me abroad; I used the opportunity to educate myself very well.

"I am extremely glad to see you, and to give billion thanks to the channel you had passed to be the person you are today, Latto. I'm proud of you, and all of our people rejoice about you," Rev. Kelikow said.

"We have a very small family with less education, opportunity, and wealth. Latto, thank the Lord that we are not sluggards, but energetic people who are resilient achievers. At least we have broadcast our family's name around the world as our late grandmother, Neh Korto once perceived. We have reminded the entire community that nothing better comes easily. We considered the many droplets of our tears, our wounded fingers, our bloody noses, our enduring excruciating hurts and they have paved the way for our success. Any life without struggle is a life not worth living as the sluggards."

Latto began to recall decades-old events. "I will never forget the day I went to sell charcoal with my mother, Suah, that day led me to my present life. I strongly believe the old folks' saying: no man passes by his luck. If he can't get it, at least the luck will surely see his face before his death. My luck saw my face that morning."

Chapter 30

The next day, Latto parked her car by her building situated at the outskirt of Christopolis. By the side of the building was Suah along with her three grandchildren, watering her vegetable garden. In the living room was Kenda, conversing with Leemu on the phone.

Later, Latto and Rev. Kelikow went to the airport and picked up Dr. Kiamu and his wife from their Euro-Afro-Asian tour. In a few hours, Captain Jerma along with his wife also joined the family from his overseas military assignment.

When it came time for dinner, Latto looked at her parents with excitement. She couldn't figure out what word to utter first.

"I'm so thankful for the care you have given me. I pray the God of this universe will reward you," she said.

"I don't think we have time for your bragging, Latto."

"Let her say what's right about us, while we are alive," Leemu said to Suah. "I don't want to be confined in my casket, waiting for eternity before she can deposit me a bouquet of flower. And, I don't think you want that, either."

"My friend, rejoice in your heart that you are alive. Counting your blessings in public means you are introducing yourself to demons. They will feast on your carcass," said Suah as she looked at her only educated daughter in a cautious way.

"Mothers are blessings to their children," Leemu said.

"All ladies are women, but not all women are mothers," Dr. Kiamu interrupted.

Leemu raised her eyebrows; "I knew you would say that against women."

"No, honey, don't get me wrong. I respect mothers," he laughed as he tapped on the back of his wife. "There is no measurement scale to measure the tons of blessings mothers can bestow on their children."

Latto understood what her father meant, he couldn't downplay ladies. She remembered how the men in her village loved their families.

"Men went to church along with their wives and children on Sundays, while others went on Saturdays and sat in the same pews with their loved ones. On the other hand, the young ladies went to fish, while the young men went to hunt. The men dined together, while their wives or suitors communally ate in the kitchen," Latto said.

"In Payeta, men were responsible for constructing bridges, clearing around the village, brushing the roads, working on the elite farms, and doing farming and hunting to support their families. Men were known for protecting their communities from internal and external aggressions. Crimes were minimized in Leewah.

"Men cherished their women and entrusted them with the responsibilities of home-decoration and childcare. The men didn't allow any other man to assault their women either in their presence or in their absence. If such was done, the punishment was either death or war against the perpetrator and his entire community.

"The women were also allowed to select their own leaders for their own little world of womanhood. They worked hand in hand with the men as partners in progress, rather than looking at women as subjects to men."

Latto understood that it was for that reason she respected Suah's view. She had always been careful and through her humility, the villagers nobly accepted her. Like her mother, Neh Korto, the villagers had selected Suah as the new chief female herbalist of the village, being licensed by the government.

As a token of appreciation to her people, Latto had a banquet on the seventy-seventh birthday of Suah. Latto thanked Manu, Leemu and Dr. Kiamu for allowing the Lord to use them as the channels of her blessings.

"I might have been born in the place that denied my generation all essential privileges unlike no others, but I surfaced on this side of the planet at the right time. No other period could have made me more proud had I denied taking advantage of all the available opportunities at the right time."

She held the banquet to teach others the unfailing love.

"Besides God, Manu is the person we must thank," said Dr. Kiamu, placing his hand on Manu's shoulder.

Then, Latto smiled and called Baby D, her first son, "Do you want to recite your poem for your grandparents?"

"Yeah," he said, smiling broadly, and he began to recite the poem:

My second god is my mother.
Who can be like my mother?
She could have taken me out,
She carefully allowed me in.
My mother is my heroine,
She gave me passion and care
She drew me out of the eagles' nest.
She turned the stones for my bread.
And furled the wind for my breath;
There's no substitute for my mother
Though we have our ups and downs,
My second god is still my mother.

"Wow! You need some kind of gift for your birthday," said Leemu as she placed Baby D on her chest. "Continue the good work. I'm proud of you."

Many friends also made encouraging remarks, thanking Latto for the way she utilized her opportunities abroad. As they continued, the day became a memorable time in their lives.

Just like on a movie screen, a panorama of Suah's previous interactions with her female colleagues in Payeta drifted through her memory. She remembered that one day a controversial woman named Gormah welcomed her colleagues under her veranda to help crack peanuts.

Suah said that Neh Gormah told friends, "Suah and her husband are battling with a failed marital relationship. In fact, none of their children is going to school. What kind of marriage is that? Right away Neh Nomon, a respectable elderly lady, interrupted Neh Gormah and rebuked her, 'what are you saying, woman? Don't you know that no rooster is free to crow in a strange basket, unless it is willing to borrow its neck to the slaughtering knife? Don't you know that living abroad is the hardest thing for many people?'

"Some of you haven't traveled; that is why you are mocking others. Even though Suah married a man from a different region, one day they will surprise you. If they don't become the people you expect them to be, one of their children will.

"One thing I believe every good parent always remembers to say, 'My child needs my blessings before I die, because nothing better comes easily for those in need.' Suah is going to be the person you have not known. Neh Gormah and her friends were abject with shame and disgrace."

After Suah's talk, the program came to an end. Suah, weighed down with an unexpected joy, lifted up her head in her rocking chair and smiled.

"Nobody, including Gormah, will overlook my family again," Suah said, "That's the reason every woman must give birth to a child or surrogate a child. As Latto came from my real body, she has washed away my shame. I will no longer have resentments for anybody for his or her mockery against my family.

"What else in this world do I care for? I have done my part. The Lord has been generous to me. I didn't deserve these blessings. At least, I am happy that people will see Latto and remember my contribution to this community," bragged Suah. "God has blessed me. I took the right step. I trekked on His blessing road that led me to good life abroad. He has answered all my desires. Through the same blessing my future generations will walk."

She knocked her chest. "Now, I can lie in my casket with a smile of success. I can happily join my gone-folks. I know they will surely be glad to welcome me." She turned to the side where Latto stood, collecting the dishes and paying less attention. She directed, "Latto, whenever I give up the ghost, please gather me into my family's resting place."

Suah lay backward and closed her feeble eyes. Dr. Kiamu, who was sitting near by her, hearing all these amazing statements, checked her pulse. He cried out, "Latto, it's unfortunate. Neh Suah is gone. She is gone. Our mother is gone, Latto."

Then, Latto threw the rest of the dishes on the floor and rushed to her father and shouted, "What do you mean by she's gone, Daddy? What has happened to her? No, no, don't tell me that! Not now, Mommy. Not now! I'm your baby. You told me that I'm your walking stick. Please, you should not leave me like this! I can't live without you!" Others joined her and they all wept.

The Author

ADVENTOR TRYE is an ordained minister and author of two novels: *Blessing Road and Jungle Justice*. He was born on October 15, 1960 in Kayata, Upper Bong County, Liberia. He attended Cuttington University, Andrews University, Northwestern College and Loft Literary Center. He had worked in West Africa and the United States. He is the incorporator of the non-profit organization of Minnesota, Life-Way Resource Center. He plans to donate a portion of the royalty from these novels toward the construction of a college of psychology and professional studies for disadvantaged young people in Liberia. He encourages you to at least purchase a copy to help eradicate ignorance. You can contact him by E-mail: kiamubillie@yahoo.com or by phone (763) 432 5609 or the publisher.

CPSIA information can be obtained at www.ICGtesting.com
224096LV00001B/2/P

9 781448 924974